Elissa by H. Rider Haggard

Sir Henry Rider Haggard, KBE was born on June 22nd, 1856 at Bradenham in Norfolk, England.

After his education he was pushed towards an Army career but failed the entrance exam. Next Haggard was positioned to work for the British Foreign Office but he seems not to have sat that exam. Using family connections, he was sent to Southern Africa by his father in search of a further opportunity of a career.

Haggard spent six years there before a return to England and marriage. He had begun to write and publish some non-fiction in Africa but it was only after studying Law in the hope it might prove to be the proper career his father wanted for him that Haggard began to write fiction, using his African experiences as the basis.

His first fiction was published in 1885 and the following year King Solomon's Mines was published. It was a phenomenal success. His career was set.

Haggard wrote well and wrote often. He managed to sympathise with the local populations even though they were exploited and manipulated by Europeans intent on amassing fortunes in money, people and resources. His writing career covered the great sprint to Empire of several European powers and both reflects and criticizes these events through his well-loved characters including Allan Quatermain and Ayesha.

In his later years Haggard pursued much in the way social reform as well as standing for Parliament and writing a great many letters to The Times.

Henry Rider Haggard died on May 14th, 1925 at the age of 68. His ashes were buried at Ditchingham Church.

Index of Contents

Note

The world is full of ruins, but few of them have an origin so utterly lost in mystery as those of Zimbabwe in South Central Africa. Who built them? What purpose did they serve? These are questions that must have perplexed many generations, and many different races of men.

The researches of Mr. Wilmot prove to us indeed that in the Middle Ages Zimbabwe or Zimboe was the seat of a barbarous empire, whose ruler was named the Emperor of Monomotapa, also that for some years the Jesuits ministered in a Christian church built beneath the shadow of its ancient towers. But of the original purpose of those towers, and of the race that reared them, the inhabitants of mediæval Monomotapa, it is probable, knew less even than we know to-day. The labours and skilled observation of the late Mr. Theodore Bent, whose death is so great a loss to all interested in such matters, have shown almost beyond question that Zimbabwe was once an inland Phoenician city, or at the least a city whose inhabitants were of a race which practised Phoenician customs and worshipped the Phoenician deities. Beyond this all is conjecture. How it happened that a trading town, protected by vast fortifications and adorned with temples dedicated to the worship of the gods of the Sidonians—or rather trading towns, for Zimbabwe is only one of a group of ruins—were built by civilised men in the heart of Africa perhaps we shall never learn with certainty, though the discovery of the burying-places of their inhabitants might throw some light upon the problem.

But if actual proof is lacking, it is scarcely to be doubted—for the numerous old workings in Rhodesia tell their own tale—that it was the presence of payable gold reefs worked by slave labour which tempted the Phoenician merchants and chapmen, contrary to their custom, to travel so far from the sea and establish themselves inland. Perhaps the city Zimboe was the Ophir spoken of in the first Book of Kings. At least, it is almost certain that its principal industries were the smelting and the sale of gold, also it seems probable that expeditions travelling by sea and land would have occupied quite three years of time in reaching it from Jerusalem and returning thither laden with the gold and precious stones, the ivory and the almug trees (1 Kings x.). Journeying in Africa must have been slow in those days; that it was also dangerous is testified by the ruins of the ancient forts built to protect the route between the gold towns and the sea.

However these things may be, there remains ample room for speculation both as to the dim beginnings of the ancient city and its still dimmer end, whereof we can guess only, when it became weakened by luxury and the mixture of races, that hordes of invading savages stamped it out of existence beneath their blood-stained feet, as, in after ages, they stamped out the Empire of Monomotapa. In the following romantic sketch the writer has ventured—no easy task—to suggest incidents such as might have accompanied this first extinction of the Phoenician Zimbabwe. The pursuit indeed is one in which he can only hope to fill the place of a humble pioneer, since it is certain that in times to come the dead fortress-temples of South Africa will occupy the pens of many generations of the writers of romance who, as he hopes, may have more ascertained facts to build upon than are available to-day.

Chapter I

The Caravan

The sun, which shone upon a day that was gathered to the past some three thousand years ago, was setting in full glory over the expanses of south-eastern Africa—the Libya of the ancients. Its last burning rays fell upon a cavalcade of weary men, who, together with long strings of camels, asses and oxen, after much toil had struggled to the crest of a line of stony hills, where they were halted to recover breath. Before them lay a plain, clothed with sere yellow grass—for the season was winter—and bounded by mountains of no great height, upon whose slopes stood the city which they had travelled far to seek. It was the ancient city of Zimboe, whereof the lonely ruins are known to us moderns as Zimbabwe.

At the sight of its flat-roofed houses of sun-dried brick, set upon the side of the opposing hill, and dominated by a huge circular building of dark stone, the caravan raised a great shout of joy. It shouted in several tongues, in the tongues of Phoenicia, of Egypt, of the Hebrews, of Arabia, and of the coasts of Africa, for all these peoples were represented amongst its numbers. Well might the wanderers cry out in their delight, seeing that at length, after eight months of perilous travelling from the coast, they beheld the walls of their city of rest, of the golden Ophir of the Bible. Their company had started from the eastern port, numbering fifteen hundred men, besides women and children, and of those not more than half were left alive. Once a savage tribe had ambushed them, killing many. Once the pestilential fever of the low lands had taken them so that they died of it by scores. Twice also had they suffered heavily through hunger and thirst, to say nothing of their losses by the fangs of lions, crocodiles, and other wild beasts which with the country swarmed. Now their toils were over; and for six months, or perhaps a year, they might rest and trade in the Great City, enjoying its wealth, its flesh-pots, and the unholy orgies which, among people of the Phoenician race, were dignified by the name of the worship of the gods of heaven.

Soon the clamour died away, and although no command was given, the caravan started on at speed. All weariness faded from the faces of the way-worn travellers, even the very camels and asses, shrunk, as most of them were, to mere skeletons, seemed to understand that labour and blows were done with, and forgetting their loads, shambled un-urged down the stony path. One man lingered, however. Clearly he was a person of rank, for eight or ten attendants surrounded him.

"Go," said he, "I wish to be alone, and will follow presently." So they bowed to the earth, and went.

The man was young, perhaps six or eight and twenty years of age. His dark skin, burnt almost to blackness by the heat of the sun, together with the fashion of his short, square-cut beard and of his garments, proclaimed him of Jewish or Egyptian blood, while the gold collar about his neck and the gold graven ring upon his hand showed that his rank was high. Indeed this wanderer was none other than the prince Aziel, nick-named the Ever-living, because of a curious mole upon his shoulder bearing a resemblance to the crux ansata, the symbol of life eternal among the Egyptians. By blood he was a grandson of Solomon, the mighty king of Israel, and born of a royal mother, a princess of Egypt.

In stature Aziel was tall, but somewhat slimly made, having small bones. His face was oval in shape, the features, especially the mouth, being fine and sensitive; the eyes were large, dark, and full of thought—the eyes of a man with a destiny. For the most part, indeed, they were sombre and over-full of thought, but at times they could light up with a strange fire.

Aziel the prince placed his hand against his forehead in such fashion as to shade his face from the rays of the setting sun, and from beneath its shadow gazed long and earnestly at the city of the hill.

"At length I behold thee, thanks be to God," he murmured, for he was a worshipper of Jehovah, and not of his mother's deities, "and it is time, since, to speak the truth, I am weary of this travelling. Now what fortune shall I find within thy walls, O City of Gold and devil- servers?"

"Who can tell?" said a quiet voice at his elbow. "Perhaps, Prince, you will find a wife, or a throne, or—a grave."

Aziel started, and turned to see a man standing at his side, clothed in robes that had been rich, but were now torn and stained with travel, and wearing on his head a black cap in shape not unlike the fez that is common in the East to-day. The man was past middle age, having a grizzled beard, sharp, hard features and quick eyes, which withal were not unkindly. He was a Phoenician merchant, much trusted by Hiram, the King of Tyre, who had made him captain of the merchandise of this expedition.

"Ah! is it you, Metem?" said Aziel. "Why do you leave your charge to return to me?"

"That I may guard a more precious charge—yourself, Prince," replied the merchant courteously. "Having brought the child of Israel so far in safety, I desire to hand him safely to the governor of yonder city. Your servants told me that by your command they had left you alone, so I returned to bear you company, for after nightfall robbers and savages wander without these walls."

"I thank you for your care, Metem, though I think there is little danger, and at the worst I can defend myself."

"Do not thank me, Prince; I am a merchant, and now, as in the past, I protect you, knowing that for it I shall be paid. The governor will give me a rich reward when I lead you to him safely, and when in years to come I return with you still safe to the court of Jerusalem, then the great king will fill my ship's hold with gifts."

"That depends, Metem," replied the prince. "If my grandfather still reigns it may be so, but he is very old, and if my uncle wears his crown, then I am not sure. Truly you Phoenicians love money. Would you, then, sell me for gold also, Metem?"

"I said not so, Prince, though even friendship has its price—"

"Among your people, Metem?"

"Among all people, Prince. You reproach us with loving money; well, we do, since money gives everything for which men strive—honour, and place, and comfort, and the friendship of kings."

"It cannot give you love, Metem."

The Phoenician laughed contemptuously. "Love! with gold I will buy as much of it as I need. Are there no slaves upon the market, and no free women who desire ornaments and ease and the purple of Tyre? You are young, Prince, to say that gold cannot buy us love."

"And you, Metem, who are growing old, do not understand what I mean by love, nor will I stay to explain it to you, for were my words as wise as Solomon's, still you would not understand. At the least your money cannot bring you the blessing of Heaven, nor the welfare of your spirit in the eternal life that is to come."

"The welfare of my spirit, Prince? No, it cannot, since I do not believe that I have a spirit. When I die, I die, and there is an end. But the blessing of Heaven, ah! that can be bought, as I have proved once and again, if not with gold, then otherwise. Did I not in bygone years pass the first son of my manhood through the fire to Baal-Sidon? Nay, shrink not from me; it cost me dear, but my fortune was at stake, and better that the boy should die than that all of us should live on in penury and bonds. Know you not, Prince, that the gods must have the gifts of the best, gifts of blood and virtue, or they will curse us and torment us?"

"I do not know it, Metem, for such gods are no gods, but devils, children of Beelzebub, who has no power over the righteous. Truly I would have none of your two gods, Phoenician; upon earth the god of gold, and in heaven the devil of slaughter."

"Speak no ill of him, Prince," answered Metem solemnly, "for here you are not in the courts of Jehovah, but in his land, and he may chance to prove his power on you. For the rest, I had sooner follow after gold than the folly of a drunken spirit which you name Love, seeing that it works its votary less mischief. Say now, it was a woman and her love that drove you hither to this wild land, was it not, Prince? Well, be careful lest a woman and her love should keep you here."

"The sun sets," said Aziel coldly; "let us go forward."

With a bow and a murmured salute, for his quick courtier instinct told him that he had spoken too freely, Metem took the bridle of the prince's mule, holding the stirrup while he mounted. Then he turned to seek his own, but the animal had wandered, and a full half hour went by before it could be captured.

By now the sun had set, and as there is little or no twilight in Southern Africa it became difficult for the two travellers to find their way down the rough hill path. Still they stumbled on, till presently the long dead grass brushing against their knees told them that they had lost the road, although they knew that they were riding in the right direction, for the watch-fires burning on the city walls were a guide to them. Soon, however, they lost sight of these fires, the boughs of a grove of thickly-leaved trees hiding them from view, and in trying to push their way through the wood Metem's mule stumbled against a root and fell.

"Now there is but one thing to be done," said the Phoenician, as he dragged the animal from the ground, "and it is to stay here till the moon rises, which should be within an hour. It would have been wiser, Prince, if we had waited to discuss love and the gods till we were safe within the walls of the city, for the end of it is that we have fallen into the hands of king Darkness, and he is the father of many evil things."

"That is so, Metem," answered the prince, "and I am to blame. Let us bide here in patience, since we must."

So, holding their mules by the bridles, they sat down upon the ground and waited in silence, for each of them was lost in his own thoughts.

Chapter II

The Grove of Baaltis

At length, as the two men sat thus silently, for the place and its gloom oppressed them, a sound broke upon the quiet of the night, that beginning with a low wail such as might come from the lips of a mourner, ended in a chant or song. The voice, which seemed close at hand, was low, rich and passionate. At times it sank almost to a sob, and at times, taking a higher note, it thrilled upon the air in tones that would have been shrill were they not so sweet.

"Who is it that sings?" said Aziel to Metem.

"Be silent, I pray you," whispered the other in his ear; "we have wandered into one of the sacred groves of Baaltis, which it is death for men to enter save at the appointed festivals, and a priestess of the grove chants her prayer to the goddess."

"We did not come of our own will, so doubtless we shall be forgiven," answered Aziel indifferently; "but that song moves me. Tell me the words of it, which I can scarcely follow, for her accent is strange to me."

"Prince, they seem to be holy words to which I have little right to hearken. The priestess sings an ancient hallowed chant of life and death, and she prays that the goddess may touch her soul with the wing of fire and make her great and give her vision of things that have been and that shall be. More I dare not tell you now; indeed I can barely hear, and the song is hard to understand. Crouch down, for the moon rises, and pray that the mules may not stir. Presently she will go, and we can fly the holy place."

The Israelite obeyed and waited, searching the darkness with eager eyes.

Now the edge of the great moon appeared upon the horizon, and by degrees her white rays of light revealed a strange scene to the watchers. About an open space of ground, some eighty paces in diameter, grew seven huge and ancient baobab trees, so ancient indeed that they must have been planted by the primæval hand of nature rather than by that of man. Aziel and his companion were hidden with their mules behind the trunk of one of these trees, and looking round it they perceived that the open space beyond the shadow of the branches was not empty. In the centre of this space stood an altar, and by it was placed the rude figure of a divinity carved in wood and painted. On the head of this figure rose a crescent symbolical of the moon, and round its neck hung a chain of wooden stars. It had four wings but no hands, and of these wings two were out-spread and two clasped a shapeless object to its breast, intended, apparently, to represent a child. By these symbols Aziel knew that before him was an effigy sacred to the goddess of the Phoenicians, who in different countries passed by the various names of Astarte, or Ashtoreth, or Baaltis, and who in their coarse worship was at once the personification of the moon and the emblem of fertility.

Standing before this rude fetish, between it and the altar, whereon lay some flowers, and in such fashion that the moonlight struck full upon her, was a white-robed woman. She was young and very beautiful both in shape and feature, and though her black hair streaming almost to the knees took from her height, she still seemed tall. Her rounded arms were outstretched; her sweet and passionate face was upturned towards the sky, and even at that distance the watchers could see her deep eyes shining in the moonlight. The sacred song of the priestess was finished. Now she was praying aloud, slowly, and in a clear voice, so that Aziel could hear and understand her; praying from her very heart, not to the idol before her, however, but to the moon above.

"O Queen of Heaven," she said, "thou whose throne I see but whose face I cannot see, hear the prayer of thy priestess, and protect me from the fate I fear, and rid me of him I hate. Safe let me dwell and pure, and as thou fillest the night with light, so fill the darkness of my soul with the wisdom that I crave. O whisper into my ears and let me hear the voice of heaven, teaching me that which I would know. Read me the riddle of my life, and let me learn wherefore I am not as my sisters are; why feasts and offerings delight me not; why I thirst for knowledge and not for wealth, and why I crave such love as here I cannot win. Satisfy my being with thy immortal lore and a love that does not fail or die, and if thou wilt, then take my life in payment. Speak to me from the heaven above, O Baaltis, or show me some sign upon the earth beneath; fill up the vessel of my thirsty soul and satisfy the hunger of my spirit. Oh! thou that art the goddess, thou that hast the gift of power, give me, thy servant, of thy power, of thy godhead, and of thy peace. Hear me, O Heaven-born, hear me, Elissa, the daughter of Sakon, the dedicate of thee. Hear, hear, and answer now in the secret holy hour, answer by voice, by wonder, or by symbol."

The woman paused as though exhausted with the passion of her prayer, hiding her face in her hands, and as she stood thus silent and expectant, the sign came, or at least that chanced which for a while she believed to have been an answer to her invocation. Her face was hidden, so she could not see, and fascinated by her beauty as it appeared to them in that unhallowed spot, and by the depth and dignity of her wild prayer, the two watchers had eyes for her alone. Therefore it happened that not until his arm was about to drag her away, did either of them perceive a huge man, black as ebony in colour, clad in a cloak of leopard skins and carrying in his right hand a broad-bladed spear who, following the shadow of the trees, had crept upon the priestess from the farther side of the glade.

With a guttural exclamation of triumph he gripped her in his left arm, and, despite her struggles and her shrill cry for help, began half to drag and half to carry her towards the deep shade of the baobab grove. Instantly Aziel and Metem sprang up and rushed forward, drawing their bronze swords as they ran. As it chanced, however, the Israelite caught his foot in one of the numerous tree-roots, which stood above the surface of the ground and fell heavily upon his face. In a few seconds, twenty perhaps, he found his breath and feet again, to see that Metem had come up with the black giant who, hearing his approach, suddenly wheeled round to meet him, still holding the struggling priestess in his grasp. Now the Phoenician was so close upon him that the savage could find no time to shift the grip upon his spear, but drove at him with the knobbed end of its handle, striking him full upon the forehead and felling him as a butcher fells an ox. Then once more he turned to fly with his captive, but before he had covered ten yards the sound of Aziel's approaching footsteps caused him to wheel round again.

At sight of the Israelite advancing upon him with drawn sword, the great barbarian freed himself from the burden of the girl by throwing her heavily to the ground, where she lay, for the breath was shaken out of her. Then snatching the cloak from his throat he wound it over his left arm to serve as a shield, and with a savage yell, rushed straight at Aziel, purposing to transfix him with the broad-headed spear.

Well was it for the prince that he had been trained in sword-play from his youth, also, notwithstanding his slight build, that he was strong and active as a leopard. To await the onslaught would be to die, for the spear must pierce him before ever he could reach the attacker's body with his short sword. Therefore, as the weapon flashed upward he sprang aside, avoiding it, at the same time, with one swift sweep of his sword, slashing its holder across the back as he passed him.

With a howl of pain and rage the savage sprang round and charged him a second time. Again Aziel leapt to one side, but now he struck with all his force at the spear shaft which his assailant lifted to guard his head. So strong was the blow and so sharp the heavy sword, that it shore through the wood, severing the handle from the spear, which fell to the ground. Casting away the useless shaft, the warrior drew a long knife from his girdle, and before Aziel could strike again faced him for the third time. But he no longer rushed onward like a bull, for he had learnt caution; he stood still, holding the skin cloak before him shield fashion, and peering at his adversary from over its edge.

Now it was Aziel's turn to take the offensive, and slowly he circled round the huge barbarian, watching his opportunity. At length it came. In answer to a feint of his, the protecting cloak was dropped a little, enabling him to prick its bearer in the neck, but only with the point of his sword. The thrust delivered, he leapt back, and not too soon, for forgetting his caution in his fury, the savage charged straight at him with a roar like that of a lion. So swift and terrible was his onset that Aziel, having no time to spring aside, did the only thing possible. Gripping the ground with his feet, he bent his body forward, and with outstretched arm and sword, braced up his muscles to receive the charge. Another instant, and the leopard skin cloak fluttered before him. With a quick movement of his left arm he swept it aside; then there came a sudden pressure upon his sword ending in a jarring shock, a flash of steel above his head, and down he went to the ground beneath the weight of the black giant.

"Now there is an end," he thought; "Heaven receive my spirit." And his senses left him.

When they returned again, Aziel perceived dimly that a white-draped figure bent over him, dragging at something black which crushed his breast, who, as she dragged, sobbed in her grief and fear. Then he remembered, and with an effort sat up, rolling from him the corpse of his foe, for his sword had pierced the barbarian through breast and heart and back. At this sight the woman ceased her sobbing, and said in the Phoenician tongue:—

"Sir, do you indeed live? Then the protecting gods be thanked, and to Baaltis the Mother I vow a gift of this hair of mine in gratitude."

"Nay, lady," he answered faintly, for he was much shaken, "that would be a pity; also, if any, it is my hair which should be vowed."

"You bleed from the head," she broke in; "say, stranger, are you deeply wounded."

"I will tell you nothing of my head," he replied, with a smile, "unless you promise that you will not offer up your hair."

"So be it, stranger, since I must; I will give the goddess this gold chain instead; it is of more worth."

"You would do better, lady," said the shrill voice of Metem again, who by now had found his wits again, "to give the gold chain to me whose scalp has been broken in rescuing you from that black thief."

"Sir," she answered, "I am grateful to you from my heart, but it is this young lord who killed the man and saved me from slavery worse than death, and he shall be rewarded by my father."

"Listen to her," grumbled Metem. "Did I not rush in first in my folly and receive what I deserved for my pains? But am I to have neither thanks nor pay, who am but an old merchant; they are for the young prince who came after. Well, so it ever was; the thanks I can spare, and the reward I shall claim from the treasury of the goddess.

"Now, Prince, let me see your hurt. Ah! a cut on the ear, no more, and thank your natal star that it is so, for another inch and the great vein of the neck would have been severed. Prince, if you are able, draw out your sword from the carcase of that brute, for I have tried and cannot loosen the blade. Then perhaps this lady will guide us to the city before his fellows come to seek him, seeing that for one night I have had a stomach full of fighting."

"Sirs, I will indeed. It is close at hand, and my father will thank you there; but if it is your pleasure, tell me by what names I shall make known to him you whose rank seems to be so high?"

"Lady, I am Metem the Phoenician, captain of the merchandise of the caravan of Hiram, King of Tyre, and this lord who slew the thief is none other than the prince Aziel, the twice royal, for he is grandson to the glorious King of Israel, and through his mother of the blood of the Pharaohs of Egypt."

"And yet he risked his life to save me," the girl murmured astonished; then dropping to her knees before Aziel, she touched the ground with her forehead in obeisance, giving him thanks, and praising him after the fashion of the East.

"Rise, lady," he broke in, "because I chance to be a prince I have not ceased to be a man, and no man could have seen you in such a plight without striking a blow on your behalf."

"No," added Metem, "none; that is, as you happen to be noble and young and lovely. Had you been old and ugly and humble, then the black man might have carried you from here to Tyre ere I risked my neck to stop him, or for the matter of that, although he will deny it, the prince either."

"Men do not often show their hearts so clearly," she answered with sarcasm. "But now, lords, I will guide you to the city before more harm befalls us, for this dead man may have companions."

"Our mules are here, lady; will you not ride mine?" asked Aziel.

"I thank you, Prince, but my feet will carry me."

"And so will mine," said Aziel, ceasing from a prolonged and fruitless effort to loosen his sword from the breast-bone of the savage, "on such paths they are safer than any beasts. Friend, will you lead my mule with yours?"

"Ay, Prince," grumbled Metem, "for so the world goes with the old; you take the fair lady for company and I a she-ass. Well, of the two give me the ass which is more safe and does not chatter."

Then they started, Aziel leaving his short sword in the keeping of the dead man.

"How are you named, lady?" he said presently, adding "or rather I need not ask; you are Elissa, the daughter of Sakon, Governor of Zimboe, are you not?"

"I am so called, though how you know it I cannot guess."

"I heard you name yourself, lady, in the prayer you made before the altar."

"You heard my prayer, Prince?" she said starting. "Do you not know that it is death to that man who hearkens to the prayer of a priestess of Baaltis, uttered in her holy grove? Still, none know it save the goddess, who sees all, therefore I beseech you for your own sake and the sake of your companion, say nothing of it in the city, lest it should come to the ears of the priests of El."

"Certainly it would have been death to you had I not chanced to hear it, having lost my way in the darkness," answered the prince laughing. "Well, since I did hear it I will add that it was a beautiful prayer, revealing a heart high and pure, though I grieve that it should have been offered to one whom I hold to be a demon."

"I am honoured," she answered coldly; "but, Prince, you forget that though you, being a Hebrew, worship Him they call Jehovah, or so I have been told, I, being of the blood of the Sidonians, worship the lady Baaltis, the Queen of Heaven the holy one of whom I am a priestess."

"So it is, alas!" he said, with a sigh, adding:—

"Well, let us not dispute of these matters, though, if you wish, the prophet Issachar, the Levite who accompanies me, can explain the truth of them to you."

Elissa made no reply, and for a while they walked on in silence.

"Who was that black robber whom I slew?" Aziel asked presently.

"I am not sure, Prince," she answered, hesitating, "but savages such as he haunt the outskirts of the city seeking to steal white women to be their wives. Doubtless he watched my steps, following me into the holy place."

"Why, then, did you venture there alone, lady?"

"Because, to be heard, such prayers as mine must be offered in solitude in the consecrated grove, and at the hour of the rising of the moon. Moreover, cannot Baaltis protect her priestess, Priest, and did she not protect her?"

"I thought, lady, that I had something to do with the matter," he answered.

"Ay, Prince, it was your hand that struck the blow which killed the thief, but Baaltis, and no other, led you to the place to rescue me."

"I understand, lady. To save you, Baaltis, laying aside her own power, led a mortal man to the grove, which it is death that mortal man should violate."

"Who can fathom the way of the gods?" she replied with passion, then added, as though reasoning with a new-born doubt, "Did not the goddess hear my prayer and answer it?"

"In truth, lady, I cannot say. Let me think. If I understood you rightly, you prayed for heavenly wisdom, but whether or not you have gained it within this last hour, I do not know. And then you prayed for love, an immortal love. O, maiden, has it come to you since yonder moon appeared upon the sky? And you prayed—"

"Peace!" she broke in, "peace and mock me not, or, prince that you are, I will publish your crime of spying upon the prayer of a priestess of Baaltis. I tell you that I prayed for a symbol and a sign, and the prayer was answered.

"Did not the black giant spring upon me to bear me away to be his slave—his, or another's? And is he not a symbol of the evil and the ignorance which are on the earth and that seek to drag down the beauty and the wisdom of the earth to their own level? Then the Phoenician ran to rescue me and was defeated, since the spirit of Mammon cannot overcome the black powers of ill. Next you came and fought hard and long, till in the end you slew the mighty foe, you a Prince born of the royal blood of the world—" and she ceased.

"You have a pretty gift of parable, lady, as it should be with one who interprets the oracles of a goddess. But you have not told me of what I, your servant, am the symbol."

She stopped in her walk and looked him full in the face.

"I never heard," she said, "that either the Jews or the Egyptians, being instructed, were blind to the reading of an allegory. But, Prince, if you cannot read this one it is not for me, who am but a woman, to set it out to you."

Just then their glances met, and in the clear moonlight Aziel saw a wave of doubt sweep over his companion's dark and beautiful eyes, and a faint flush appear upon her brow. He saw, and something stirred at his heart that till this hour he had never felt, something which even now he knew it would trouble him greatly to escape.

"Tell me, lady," he asked, his voice sinking almost to a whisper, "in this fable of yours am I even for an hour deemed worthy to play the part of that immortal love embodied which you sought so earnestly a while ago?"

"Immortal love, Prince," she answered, in a new voice, a voice low and deep, "is not for one hour, but for all hours that are and are to be. You, and you alone, can know if you would dare to play such a part as this—even in a fable."

"Perchance, lady, there lives a woman for whom it might be dared."

"Prince, no such woman lives, since immortal love must deal, not with the flesh, but with the spirit. If a spirit worthy to be thus loved and worshipped now wanders in earthly shape upon the world, seeking its counterpart and its completion, I cannot tell. Yet were it so, and should they chance to meet, it might be happy for such brave spirits, for then the answer to the great riddle would be theirs."

Wondering what this riddle might be, Aziel bent towards her to reply, when suddenly round a bend in the path but a few paces from them came a body of soldiers and attendants, headed by a man clad in a white robe and walking with a staff. This man was grey-headed and keen-eyed, thin in face and ascetic in appearance, with a brow of power and a bearing of dignity. At the sight of the pair he halted, looking at them in question, and with disapproval.

"Our search is ended," he said in Hebrew, "for here is he whom we seek, and alone with him a heathen woman, robed like a priestess of the Groves."

"Whom do you seek, Issachar?" asked Aziel hurriedly, for the sudden appearance of the Levite disturbed him.

"Yourself, Prince. Surely you can guess that your absence has been noted. We feared lest harm should have come to you, or that you had lost your path, but it seems that you have found a guide," and he stared at his companion sternly.

"That guide, Issachar," answered Aziel, "being none other than the lady Elissa, daughter of Sakon, governor of this city, and our host, whom it has been my good fortune to rescue from a woman-stealer yonder in the grove of the goddess Baaltis."

"And whom it was my bad fortune to try to rescue in the said grove, as my broken head bears witness," added Metem, who by now had come up, dragging the two mules after him.

"In the grove of the goddess Baaltis!" broke in the Levite with a kindling eye, and striking the ground with his staff to emphasise his words. "You, a Prince of Israel, alone in the high place of abomination with the priestess of a fiend? Fie upon you, fie upon you! Would you also walk in the sin of your forefathers, Aziel, and so soon?"

"Peace!" said Aziel in a voice of command; "I was not in the grove alone or by my own will, and this is no time or place for insults and wrangling."

"Between me and those who seek after false gods, or the women who worship them, there is no peace," replied the old priest fiercely.

Then, followed by all the company, he turned and strode towards the gates of the city.

Chapter III

Ithobal the King

Two hours had gone by, and the prince Aziel, together with his retinue, the officers of the caravan, and many other guests, were seated at a great feast made in their honour, by Sakon, the governor of the city. This feast was held in the large pillared hall of Sakon's house, built beneath the northern wall of the temple fortress, and not more than a few paces from its narrow entrance, through which in case of alarm the inhabitants of the palace could fly for safety. All down this chamber were placed tables, accommodating more than two hundred feasters, but the principal guests were seated by themselves upon a raised daïs at the head of the hall. Among them sat Sakon himself, a middle-aged man stout in build, and thoughtful of face, his daughter Elissa, some other noble ladies, and a score or more of the notables of the city and its surrounding territories.

One of these strangers immediately attracted the attention of Aziel, who was seated in the place of honour at the right of Sakon, between him and the lady Elissa. This man was of large stature, and about forty years of age; the magnificence of his apparel and the great gold chain set with rough diamonds which hung about his neck showing him to be a person of importance. His tawny complexion marked him of mixed race. This conclusion his features did not belie, for the brow, nose, and cheek-bones were Semitic in outline, while the full, prominent eyes, and thick, sensuous lips could with equal certainty be attributed to the Negroid stock. In fact, he was the son of a native African queen, or chieftainess, and a noble Phoenician, and his rank no less than that of absolute king and hereditary chief of a vast and undefined territory which lay around the trading cities of the white men, whereof Zimboe was the head and largest. Aziel noticed that this king, who was named Ithobal, seemed angry and ill at ease, whether because he was not satisfied with the place which had been allotted to him at the table, or for other reasons, he could not at the time determine.

When the meats had been removed, and the goblets were filled with wine, men began to talk, till presently Sakon called for silence, and rising, addressed Aziel:—

"Prince," he said, "in the name of this great and free city—for free it is, though we acknowledge the king of Tyre as our suzerain—I give you welcome within our gates. Here, far in the heart of Libya, we have heard of the glorious and wise king, your grandfather, and of the mighty Pharaoh of Egypt, whose blood runs also within your veins. Prince, we are honoured in your coming, and for the asking, whatever this land of gold can boast is yours. Long may you live; may the favour of those gods you worship attend you, and in the pursuit of wisdom, of wealth, of war, and of love, may the good grain of all be garnered in your bosom, and the wind of prosperity winnow out the chaff of them to fall beneath your feet. Prince, I have greeted you as it behoves me to greet the blood of Solomon and Pharaoh; now I add a word. Now I greet you as a father greets the man who has saved his only and beloved daughter from death, or shameful bondage. Know you, friends, what this stranger did since to-night's moonrise? My daughter was at worship alone yonder without the walls, and a great savage set on her, purposing to bear her away captive. Ay, and he would have done it had not the prince Aziel here given him battle, and, after a fierce fight, slain him."

"No great deed to kill a single savage," broke in the king Ithobal, who had been listening with impatience to Sakon's praises of this high-born stranger.

"No great deed you say, King," answered Sakon. "Guards, being in the body of the man and set it before us."

There was a pause, till presently six men staggered up the hall bearing between them the corpse of the barbarian, which, still covered with the leopard skin mantle, they threw down on the edge of the daïs.

"See!" said one of the bearers, withdrawing the cloak from the huge body. Then pointing to the sword which still transfixed it, he added, "and learn what strength heaven gives to the arms of princes."

Such as the guests as were near enough rose to look at the grizzly sight, then turned to offer their congratulations to the conqueror. but there was one of them—the king Ithobal—who offered none; indeed, as his eyes fell upon the face of the corpse, they grew alight with rage.

"What ails you, King? Are you jealous of such a blow?" asked Sakon, watching him curiously.

"Speak no more of that thrust, I pray you," said Aziel, "for it was due to the weight of the man rushing on the sword, which after he was dead I could not find the power to loosen from his breast-bone."

"Then I will do you that service, Prince," sneered Ithobal, and, setting his foot upon the breast of the corpse, with a sudden effort of his great frame, he plucked out the sword and cast it down upon the table.

"Now, one might think," said Aziel, flushing with anger, "that you, King, who do a courtesy to a man of smaller strength, mean a challenge. Doubtless, however, I am mistaken, who do not understand the manners of this country."

"Think what you will, Prince," answered the chieftain, "but learn that he who lies dead before us by your hand—as you say—was no slave to be killed at pleasure, but a man of rank, none other, indeed, than the son of my mother's sister."

"Is it so?" replied Aziel, "then surely, King, you are well rid of a cousin, however highly born, who made it his business to ravish maidens from their homes."

By way of answer to these words Ithobal sprang from his seat again, laying hand upon his sword. But before he could speak or draw it, the governor Sakon addressed him in a cold and meaning voice:—

"Of your courtesy, King," he said, "remember that the prince here is my guest, as you are, and give us peace. If that dead man was your cousin, at least he well deserved to die, not at the hand of one of royal blood, but by that of the executioner, for he was the worst of thieves—a thief of women. Now tell me, King, I pray you, how came your cousin here, so far from home, since he was not numbered in your retinue?"

"I do not know, Sakon," answered Ithobal, "and if I knew I would not say. You tell me that my dead kinsman was a thief of women, which, in Phoenician eyes, must be a crime indeed. So be it; but thief or no thief, I say that there is a blood feud between me and the man who slew him, and were he great Solomon himself, instead of one of fifty princelets of his line, he should pay bitterly for the dead. To-morrow, Sakon, I will meet you before I leave for my own land, for I have words to speak to you. Till then, farewell!"—and rising, he strode down the hall, followed by his officers and guard.

The sudden departure of king Ithobal in anger was the signal for the breaking up of the feast.

"Why is that half-bred chief so wrath with me?" asked Aziel in a low voice of Elissa as they followed Sakon to another chamber.

"Because—if you would know the truth—he set his dead cousin to kidnap me, and you thwarted him," she answered, looking straight before her.

Aziel made no reply, for at that moment Sakon turned to speak with him, and his face was anxious.

"I crave your pardon, Prince," he said, drawing him aside, "that you should have met with such insults at my board. Had it been any other man who spoke thus to you, by now he had rued his words, but this Ithobal is the terror of our city, for if he chooses he can bring a hundred thousand savages upon us, shutting us within our walls to starve, and cutting us off from the working of the mines whence we win gold. Therefore, in this way or that, he must be humoured, as indeed we have humoured him and his father for years, though now," he added, his brow darkening, "he demands a price that I am loth to pay," and he glanced towards his daughter, who stood watching them at a little distance, looking most beautiful in her white robes and ornaments of gold.

"Can you not make war upon him, and break his power?" asked Aziel, with a strange anxiety, guessing that this price demanded by Ithobal was none other than Elissa, the woman whom he had rescued, and whose wisdom and beauty had stirred his heart.

"It might be done, Prince, but the risk would be great, and we are here to work the mines and grow rich in trade—not to make war. The policy of Zimboe has always been a policy of peace."

"I have a better and cheaper plan," said a calm voice at his elbow— that of Metem. "It is this: Slip a bow-string over the brute's head as he lies snoring, and pull it tight. An eagle in a cage is easy to deal with, but once on the wing the matter is different."

"There is wisdom in your counsel," said Sakon, in a hesitating voice.

"Wisdom!" broke in Aziel; "ay, the wisdom of the assassin. What, noble Sakon, would you murder a sleeping guest?"

"No, Prince, I would not," he answered hastily; "also, such a deed would bring the Tribes upon us."

"Then, Sakon, you are more foolish than you used to be," said Metem laughing. "A man who will not despatch a foe, whenever he can catch him, by means fair or foul, is not the man to govern a rich city set in the heart of a barbarous land, and so I shall tell Hiram, our king, if ever I live to see Tyre again. As for you, most high Prince, forgive the humblest of your servants if he tells you that the tenderness of your heart and the nobility of your sentiments will, I think, bring you to an early and evil end;" and, glancing towards Elissa as though to put a point upon his words, Metem smiled sarcastically and withdrew.

At this moment a messenger, whose long white hair, wild eyes and red robe announced him to be a priest of El, by which name the people of Zimboe worshipped Baal, entered the room, and whispered something into the ear of Sakon which seemed to disturb him much.

"Pardon me, Prince, and you, my guests, if I leave you," said the governor, "but I have evil tidings that call me to the temple. The lady Baaltis is seized with the black fever, and I must visit her. For an hour, farewell."

This news caused consternation among the company, and in the general confusion that followed its announcement Aziel joined Elissa, who had passed on to the balcony of the house, and was seated there alone, looking out over the moonlit city and the plains beyond. At his approach she rose in token of respect, then sat herself down again, motioning him to do likewise.

"Give me of your wisdom, lady," he said. "I thought that Baaltis was the goddess whom I heard you worshipping yonder in the grove; how, then, can she be stricken with a fever?"

"She is the goddess," Elissa answered smiling; "but the lady Baaltis is a woman whom we revere as the incarnation of that goddess upon earth, and being but a woman in her hour she must die."

"Then, what becomes of the incarnation of the goddess?"

"Another is chosen by the college of the priests of El, and the company of the priestesses of Baaltis. If that lady Baaltis who is dead chances to leave a daughter, it is usual for the lot to fall upon her; if not, upon such one of the noble maidens as may be chosen."

"Does the lady Baaltis marry, then?"

"Yes, Prince, within a year of her consecration, she must choose herself a husband, and he may be whom she will, provided only that he is of white blood, and does public sacrifice to El and Baaltis. Then after she has named him, this husband takes the title of Shadid, and for so long as his wife shall live he is the high priest of the god El, and clothed with the majesty of the god, as his wife is clothed with the majesty of Baaltis. But should she die, another wins his place."

"It is a strange faith," said Aziel, "which teaches that the Lord of Heaven can find a home in mortal breasts. But, lady, it is yours, so of it I say no more. Now tell me, if you will, what did you mean when you said that this barbarian king, Ithobal, set the savage whom I slew to kidnap you? Do you know this, or do you suspect it only?"

"I suspected it from the first, Prince, and for good reasons; moreover, I read it in the king's face as he looked upon the corpse, and when he perceived me among the feasters."

"And why should he wish to carry you away this brutally, lady, when he is at peace with the great city?"

"Perchance, Prince, after what passed to-night you can guess," she answered lowering her eyes.

"Yes, lady, I can guess, and though it is shameful that such an one should dare to think of you, still, since he is a man, I cannot blame him overmuch. But why should he press his suit in this rough and secret fashion instead of openly as a king might do?"

"He may have pressed it openly and been repulsed," she replied in a low voice. "But if he could have carried me to some far fortress, how should I flout him there, that is, if I still lived? There, with no price to pay in gold or lands or power, he would have been my master, and I should have been his slave till such time as he wearied of me. That is the fate from which you have saved me, Prince, or rather from death, for I am not one who could bear such shame at the hands of a man I hate."

"Lady," he said bowing, "I think that perhaps for the first time in my life I am glad to-night that I was born."

"And I," she answered, "who am but a Phoenician maiden, am glad that I should have lived to hear one who is as royal in thought and soul as he is in rank speak thus to me. Oh! Prince," she added, clasping her hands, "if your words are not those of empty courtesy alone, hear me, for you are great, a Lord of the Earth whom none refuse, and it may be in your power to give me aid. Prince, I am in a sore strait, for that danger from which I prayed to be delivered this night presses me hard. Prince, it is true that Ithobal has been refused my hand, both by myself and by my father, and therefore it was that he strove to steal me away. But the evil is not done with, for the great nobles of the city and the chief priests of El came to my father at sunset and prayed him that he would let Ithobal take me, seeing that otherwise in his rage he will make war upon Zimboe. When a man placed as is my father must choose between the safety of thousands and the honour and happiness of one poor girl, what will his answer be, think you?"

"Now," said Aziel, "save that no wrong can right a wrong, I almost grieve that I cried shame upon the counsel of Metem. Sweet lady, be sure of this, that I will give all I have, even to my life, to protect you from the vile fate you dread—yes, all I have—except my soul."

"Ah!" she cried with a sudden flash of her dark eyes, "all except your soul. If we women could find the man who would risk both life and soul for us, then, were he but a slave, we would worship him as never man was worshipped since Baaltis mounted her heavenly throne."

"Were I not a Hebrew you would tempt me, lady," Aziel answered smiling, "but being one I may not risk my soul even were such a prize within my reach."

"Nay, Prince," she broke in, "I did but jest; forget my words, for they were wrung from a heart torn with fears. Oh! did you know the terror of this half-savage Ithobal which oppresses me, you would forgive me all—a terror that to-night lies upon me with a tenfold weight."

"Why so, lady?"

"Doubtless because it is nearer," Elissa whispered, but her beautiful pleading eyes and quivering lips seemed to belie her words and say, "because you are near, and a change has come upon me."

For the second time that day Aziel's glance met hers, and for the second time a strange new pang that was more pain than joy, and yet half-divine, snatched at his heart-strings, for a while numbing his reason and taking from him the power of speech.

"What was it?" he wondered vaguely. He had seen many lovely faces, and many noble women had shown him favour, but why had none of them stirred him thus? Could it be that this stranger Gentile maiden was his soul-mate—she whom he was destined to love above all upon the earth, nay, whom he did already love, and so soon?

"Lady," he said, taking a step towards her, "lady—" and he paused.

Elissa bowed her dark head till her gold-bedecked and scented hair almost fell upon his feet, but she made no answer.

Then another voice broke upon the silence, a clear, strident voice that said:—

"Prince, forgive me, if for the second time to-day I disturb you; but the guests have gone; your chamber is made ready, and, not knowing the customs of the women of this country, I sought you, little guessing that, at such an hour, I should find you alone with one of them."

Aziel looked up, although there was no need for him to do so, for he knew that voice well, to see the tall form of the Levite Issachar standing before them, a cold light of anger shining in his eyes.

Elissa saw also, and, with some murmured words of farewell, she turned and went, leaving them together.

Chapter IV

The Dream of Issachar

For a moment there was silence, which Aziel broke, saying:—

"It seems to me, Issachar, that you are somewhat over zealous for my welfare."

"I think otherwise, Prince," replied the Levite sternly. "Did not your grandsire give you into my keeping, and shall I not be faithful to my trust, and to a higher duty than any which he could lay upon me?"

"Your meaning, Issachar?"

"It is plain, Prince; but I will set it out. The great king said to me yonder in the hall of his golden palace at Jerusalem, 'To others, men of war, I have given charge of the body of my grandson to keep him safe. To you, Issachar the Levite, who have fostered him, I give charge over his soul to keep it safe—a higher task, and more difficult. Guard him, Issachar, from the temptation of strange doctrines and the whisperings of strange gods, but guard him most of all from the wiles of strange women who bow the knee to Baal, for such are the gate of Gehenna upon earth, and those who enter by it shall find their place in Tophet.'"

"Truly my grandsire speaks wisely on this matter as on all others," answered Aziel, "but still I do not understand."

"Then I will be more clear, Prince. How comes it that I find you alone with this beautiful sorceress, this worshipper of the she-devil, Baaltis, with whom you should scorn even to speak, except such words as courtesy demands?"

"Is it then forbidden to me," asked Aziel angrily, "to talk with the daughter of my host, a lady whom I chanced to save from death, of the customs of her country and the mysteries of worship?"

"The mysteries of worship!" answered Issachar scornfully. "Ay! the mysteries of the worship of that fair body of hers, that ivory chalice filled with foulness—whereof, if a man drink, his faith shall be rotted and his soul poisoned. The mysteries of that worship was it, Prince, that caused you but now to lean towards this woman as though to embrace her, with words of love burning in your heart if not between your lips? Ah! these witches of Baaltis know their trade well; they are full of evil gifts, and of the wisdom given to them by the fiend they serve. With touch and sigh and look they can stir the blood of youth, having much practice in the art, till it seethes within the veins and drowns conscience in its flood.

"Nay, Prince, hear the truth," continued Issachar. "Till moonrise you had never seen this woman, and now your quick blood is aflame, and you love her. Deny it if you can—deny it on your honour and I will believe you, for you are no liar."

Aziel thought for a moment and answered:—

"Issachar, you have no right to question me on this matter, yet since you have adjured me by my honour, I will be open with you. I do not know if I love this woman, who, as you say, is a stranger to me, but it is true that my heart turns towards her like flowers to the sun. Till to-day I had never seen her, yet when my eyes first fell upon her face yonder in that accursed grove, it seemed to me that I had been born only that I might find her. It seemed to me even that for ages I had known her, that for ever she was mine and that I was hers. Read me the riddle, Issachar? Is this but passion born of youth and the sudden sight of a fair woman? That cannot be, for I have known others as fair, and have passed through some such fires. Tell me, Issachar, you who are old and wise and have seen much of the hearts of men, what is this wave that overwhelms me?"

"What is it, Prince? It is witchery; it is the wile of Beelzebub waiting to snatch your soul, and if you hearken to it you shall pass through the fire—through the fire to Moloch, if not in the flesh, then in the spirit, which is to all eternity. Oh! not in vain do I fear for you, my son, and not without reason was I warned in a dream. Listen: Last night, as I lay in my tent yonder upon the plain, I dreamed that some danger overshadowed you, and in my sleep I prayed that your destiny might be revealed to me. As I prayed thus, I heard a voice saying, 'Issachar, you seek to learn the future; know then that he who is dear to you shall be tried in the furnace indeed. Yes, because of his great love and pity, he shall forswear his faith, and with death and sorrow he shall pay the price of his sin.'

"Then I was troubled and besought Heaven that you, my son, might be saved from this unknown temptation, but the voice answered me:—

"'Of their own will only can they who were one from the beginning be held apart. Through good and ill let them work each other's woe or weal. The goal is sure, but they must choose the road.'

"Now as I wondered what these dark sayings might mean, the gloom opened and I saw you, Aziel, standing in a grove of trees, while towards you with outstretched hands drew a veiled woman who bore upon her brow the golden bow of Baaltis. Then fire raged about you, and in the fire I beheld many things which I have forgotten, and moving through it was the Prince of Death, who slew and slew and spared not. So I awoke heavy at heart, knowing that there had fallen on me who love you a shadow of doom to come."

In these latter days any educated man would set aside Issachar's wild vision as the vapourings of a mind distraught. But Aziel lived in the time of Solomon, when men of his nation guided their steps by the light of prophecy, and believed that it was the Divine pleasure, by means of dreams and wonders and through the mouths of chosen seers, to declare the will of Jehovah upon earth. To this faith, indeed, we still hold fast, at least so far as that period and people are concerned, seeing that we acknowledge

Isaiah, David, and their company, to have been inspired from above. Of that company Issachar the Levite was one, for to him, from his youth up, voices had spoken in the watches of the night, and often he had poured his warnings and denunciations into the ears of kings and peoples, telling them with no uncertain voice of the consequences of sin and idolatry, and of punishment to come. This Aziel, who had been his ward and pupil, knew well, and therefore he did not mock at the priest's dream or set it aside as naught, but bowed his head and listened.

"I am honoured indeed," he said with humility, "that the destiny of my poor soul and body should be a thing of weight to those on high."

"Of your poor soul, Aziel?" broke in Issachar. "That soul of yours, of which you speak so lightly, is of as great value in the eyes of Heaven as that of any cherubim within its gates. The angels who fell were the first and chiefest of the angels, and though now we are clad with mortal shape in punishment of our sins, again redeemed and glorified we can become among the mightiest of their hosts. Oh! my son, I beseech you, turn from this woman while there yet is time, lest to you her lips should be a cup of woe and your soul shall pay the price of them, sharing the hell of the worshippers of Ashtoreth."

"It may be so," said Aziel; "but, Issachar, what said the voice? That this, the woman of your dream and I were one from the beginning? Issachar, you believe that the lady Elissa is she of whom the voice spoke in your sleep and you bid me turn from her because she will bring me sin and punishment. In truth, if I can, I will obey you, since rather than forswear my faith, as your dream foretold, I would die a hundred deaths. Nor do I believe that for any bribe of woman's love I shall forswear it in act or thought. Yet if such things come about it is fate that drives me on, not my will—and what man can flee his fate? But even though this lady be she whom I am doomed to love, you say that because she is heathen I must reject her. Shame upon the thought, for if she is heathen it is through ignorance, and it may be mine to change her heart. Because I stand in danger shall I suffer her who, as you tell me, was one with me from the beginning, to be lost in that hell of Baal of which you speak? Nay, your dream is false. I will not renounce my faith, but rather will win her to share it, and together we shall triumph, and that I swear to you, Issachar."

"Truly the evil one has many wiles," answered the Levite, "and I did ill to tell you of my dream, seeing that it can be twisted to serve the purpose of your madness. Have your will, Aziel, and reap the fruit of it, but of this I warn you—that while I can find a way to thwart it, never, Prince, shall you take that witch to your bosom to be the ruin of your life and soul."

"Then, Issachar, on this matter there may be war between us!"

"Ay! there is war," said the Levite, and left him.

The sun was already high in the heavens when Aziel awoke from the deep and dreamless sleep which followed on the excitements and exhaustion of the previous day. After his servants had waited upon him and robed him, bringing him milk and fruit to eat, he dismissed them, and sat himself down by the casement of his chamber to think a while.

Below him lay the city of flat-roofed houses enclosed with a double wall, without the ring of which were thousands of straw huts, shaped like bee-hives, wherein dwelt natives of the country, slaves or servants of the occupying Phoenician race. To Aziel's right, and not more than a hundred paces from the governor's house in which he was, rose the round and mighty battlements of the temple, where the followers of El and Baaltis worshipped, and the gold refiners carried on their business. At intervals on its flat-topped walls stood towers of observation, alternating with pointed monoliths of granite and soapstone columns supporting vultures, rudely carved emblems of Baaltis. Between these towers armed soldiers walked continually, watching the city below and the plain beyond, for though the mission of the Phoenicians here was one of peaceful gain it was evident that they considered it necessary to be always prepared for war. On the hillside above the great temple towered another fortress of stone—a citadel deemed to be impregnable even should the temple fall into the hands of an enemy—while on the crest of the precipitous slope, stretching as far to right and left as the eye could reach, were many smaller detached strongholds.

The scene that Aziel saw from his window was a busy one, for beneath him a market was being held in an open square in the city. Here, sheltered from the sun by grass-thatched booths, the Phoenician merchants who had been his companions in their long and perilous journey from the coast were already in treaty with numerous customers, hoping, not in vain, to recoup themselves amply for the toils and dangers which they had survived. Beneath these booths were spread their goods; silks from Cos, bronze weapons and copper rods, or ingots from the rich mines of Cyprus, linens and muslins from Egypt; beads, idols, carven bowls, knives, glass ware, pottery in all shapes, and charms made of glazed faience or Egyptian stone; bales of the famous purple cloth of Tyre; surgical instruments, jewellery, and objects of toilet; scents, pots of rouge, and other unguents for the use of ladies in little alabaster and earthenware vases; bags of refined salt, and a thousand other articles of commerce produced or stored in the workshops of Phoenicia. These the chapmen bartered for raw gold by weight, tusks of ivory, ostrich feathers, and girls of approved beauty, slaves taken in war, or in some instances maidens whom their unnatural parents or relatives did not scruple to sell into bondage.

In another portion of the square, provisions and stock, alive and dead, were being offered for sale, for the most part by natives of the country. Here were piles of vegetables and fruits grown in the gardens, sacks of various sorts of grain, bundles of green forage from the irrigated lands without the walls, calabashes full of curdled milk, thick native beer and trusses of reed for thatching. Here again were oxen, mules and asses, or great bucks such as we now know as eland or kudoo, carried in on rough litters of boughs to be disposed of by parties of savage huntsmen who had shot them with arrows or trapped them in pitfalls. Every Eastern tribe and nation seemed to be represented in the motley crowd. Yonder stalked savages, naked except for their girdles, and armed with huge spears, who gazed with bewilderment on the wonders of this mart of the white man; there moved grave, long-bearded Arab merchants or Phoenicians in their pointed caps, or bare-headed white-robed Egyptians, or half-bred mercenaries clad in mail. Their variety was without end, while from them came a very babel of different tongues as they cried their wares, bargained and quarrelled.

Aziel gazed at this novel sight with interest, till, as he was beginning to weary of it, the crowd parted to right and left, leaving a clear lane across the market-place to the narrow gate of the temple. Along this lane advanced a procession of the priests of El clad in red robes, with tall red caps upon their heads, beneath which their straight hair hung down to their shoulders. In their hands were gilded rods, and round their necks hung golden chains, to which were attached emblems of the god they worshipped. They walked two-and-two to the number of fifty, chanting a melancholy dirge, one hand of each priest resting upon his fellow's shoulder, and as they passed, with the exception of certain Jews, all the spectators uncovered, while some of the more pious of them even fell upon their knees.

After the priests came a second procession, that of the priestesses of Baaltis. These women, who numbered at least a hundred, were clad in white, and wore upon their heads a gauze-like veil that fell to the knees, and was held in place by a golden fillet surmounted with the symbol of a crescent moon. Instead of the golden rods, however, each of them held in her left hand a growing stalk of maize, from the sheathed cob of which hung the bright tassel of its bloom. On her right wrist, moreover, a milk-white dove was fastened by a wire, both corn and dove being tokens of that fertility which, under various guises, was the real object of worship of these people. The sight of these white-veiled women about whose crescent-decked brows the doves fluttered, wildly striving to be free, was very strange and beautiful as they advanced also singing a low and melancholy chant. Aziel searched their faces with his eyes while they passed slowly towards him, and presently his heart bounded, for there among them, clasping the dove she bore to her breast, as though to still its frightened strugglings, was the Lady Elissa. He noticed, too, that as she went beneath the palace walls, she glanced at the window-place of his chamber, but without seeing him for he was seated in the shadow.

Presently the long line of priestesses, followed by hundreds of worshippers, had vanished through the tortuous and narrow entrance of the temple, and Aziel leaned back to think.

There, among the principal votaries of a goddess, the wickedness of whose worship was a scandal and a by-word even in the ancient world, walked the woman to whom he felt so strangely drawn and with whom, if there were any truth in the visions of Issachar and the mysterious warnings of his own soul, his fate was intertwined. As he thought of it a sudden revulsion filled his heart. She was wise and beautiful, and she seemed innocent, but Issachar was right; this girl was the minister of an abominable creed; nay, for aught he knew, she was herself defiled with its abominations, and her wisdom but an evil gift from the evil powers she served. Could he, a prince of the royal blood of the House of Israel and of the ancient Pharaohs of Khem, desire to have anything to do with such an one, he a child of the Chosen People, a worshipper of the true and only God? Yesterday she had thrown a spell upon him, a spell of black magic, or the spell of her imperial beauty, which, it mattered not, but to-day he was the lord of his own mind, and would shake himself free of it and her.

In the market-place below, the Levite Issachar also had watched the passing of the priests and priestesses of El and Baaltis.

"Tell me, Metem," he asked of the Phoenician who stood beside him, his head respectfully uncovered, "what mummery is this?"

"It is no mummery, worthy Issachar, but a ceremony of public sacrifice, which is to be offered in the temple yonder, for the recovery from her sickness of the Lady Baaltis, the high-priestess."

"Where then is the offering. I see none, unless it be those doves that are tied to the wrists of the women?"

"Nay, Issachar," answered Metem smiling darkly, "the gods ask nobler blood than that of doves. The offering is within, and it is the first- born child of a priestess of Baaltis."

"O Lord of Heaven!" said Issachar lifting up his eyes, "how long will you suffer that this murderous and accursed race should defile the face of earth?"

"Softly, friend," broke in Metem, "I have read your Scriptures, and is it not set out in them that your great forefather was commanded to offer up his first-born in such a sacrifice?"

"Blaspheme not," answered the Jew. "He was commanded indeed, that his heart might be proved, but his hand was stayed. He Whom I worship delights not in the blood of children."

Here Issachar broke off, suddenly recognising the lady Elissa among the white-robed priestesses. Watching her, he noted her glance at the window of Aziel's chamber, and saw what she could not see, that the prince was seated there. "This daughter of Satan spreads her nets," he muttered between his teeth. Then a thought struck him, and he added aloud, "Say, Metem, is it permitted to strangers to witness the rites in yonder temple?"

"Surely," answered the Phoenician; "that is, if they guard their tongues, and do nothing to offend."

"Then I desire to see them, Metem, and so doubtless does the prince Aziel. Therefore, if it is your will, do me the service to enter his chamber in the palace where he is sitting, and bid him to a great ceremony that goes forward in the temple. And, Metem, if he asks what that ceremony is, I charge you, say only that a dove is to be sacrificed.

"I will wait for you at the gate of the temple, but do not tell him that I send you on this errand. Metem, you love gain; remember that if you humour me in this and other matters which may arise, doing my bidding faithfully, I have the treasury of Jerusalem to draw upon."

"No ill paymaster," replied Metem cheerfully. "Certainly I will obey you in all things, holy Issachar, as the king commanded me yonder in Judea."

"Now," he reflected to himself, as he went upon his message, "I see how the bird flies. The prince Aziel is in love with the lady Elissa, or far upon the road to it, as at his age it is right and proper that he should be, after a twelve months' journey by sea and land with never a pretty face to sigh for. The holy Issachar, on the other hand, is minded that his charge shall have naught to do with a priestess of Baaltis, as, his age and calling considered, is also right and proper. Then there is that black savage Ithobal, who wishes to win the girl, and the girl herself, who after the fashion of her sex, will probably play them all off one against the other. Well, so much the better for me, since I shall be a richer man even than I am before this affair is done with. I have two hands, and gold is gold whoever be the giver," and smiling craftily to himself Metem passed into the palace.

Chapter V

The Place of Sacrifice

Suddenly Aziel, looking up from his reverie, saw the Phoenician bowing before him, cap in hand.

"May the Prince live for ever," he said, "yet if he suffer melancholy to overcome him thus, his life, however long, will be but sad."

"I was only thinking, Metem," answered Aziel with a start.

"Of the lady Elissa, whom you rescued, Prince? Ah! I guessed as much. She is beautiful, is she not—I have never seen the equal of those dreamy eyes and that mysterious smile—and learned also, though myself, in a woman I prefer the beauty without the learning. It is a pity now that she should chance to be a priestess of our worship, for that will not please the holy Issachar whom, I fear, Prince, you find a stern guide for the feet of youth."

"Your business, merchant?" broke in Aziel.

"I crave your pardon, Prince," answered the Phoenician, spreading out his hands in deprecation. "I struck a good bargain for my wares this morning, and drank wine to seal it, therefore, let me be forgiven if I have spoken too freely in your presence, Prince. This is my business: Yonder in the temple they celebrate a service which it is lawful for strangers to witness, and as the opportunity is rare, I thought that, having heard something of our mysteries in the grove last night, you might wish to see the office. If this be so, I am come to guide you."

"Aziel's first impulse was to refuse to go; indeed, the words of dismissal were on his lips when another purpose entered his mind. For this once he would look upon these abominations and learn what part Elissa played in them, and thus be cured for ever of the longings that had seized him.

"What is the ceremony?" he asked.

"A sacrifice for the recovery of the lady Baaltis who is sick, Prince."

"And what is the sacrifice?" asked Aziel.

"A dove, as I am told," was the indifferent answer.

"I will come with you, Metem."

"So be it, Prince. Your retinue awaits you at the gate."

At the main entrance to the palace Aziel found his guard and other servants gathered there to escort him. With them was Issachar, whom he greeted, asking him if he knew the errand upon which they were bent.

"I do, Prince; it is to witness the abomination of a sacrifice of these heathens."

"Will you then accompany me there, Issachar?"

"Where my lord goes I go," answered the Levite gravely. "Moreover, Prince, if you have your reasons for wishing to see this devil- worship, I may have mine."

Then they set out, Metem guiding them. At the north gate of the temple, which was not more than a yard in width, the Phoenician spoke to the guards on duty, who drew back to let them pass. In single file, for the passages were too narrow to allow of any other means of progression, they threaded the tortuous and mazy paths of the great building, passing between huge walls built of granite blocks laid without mortar, till at length they reached a large open space. Here the ceremony had already begun. Almost in the centre of this space, which was paved with blocks of granite, stood two conical towers, the larger of which measured thirty feet in height and the smaller about half as much. These towers, also build of blocks of stone, were, as Metem informed them, sacred to and emblematical of the gods El and

Baaltis. In front of them was a platform surmounted by a stone altar, and between them, built in a pit in the ground, burned a great furnace of wood. All the centre of the enclosure was occupied by the marshalled ranks of the priests and priestesses. Without this sacred ring stood the closely packed masses of spectators, amongst whom Aziel and his following were given place, though some of the more pious worshippers murmured audibly at the admission of these Jews.

When they entered, the companies of priests and priestesses were finishing a prayer, the sentences of which they chanted alternately with strange effect. In part it was formal, and in part an improvised supplication to the protecting gods to restore health to that woman or high-priestess who was known as the lady Baaltis. The prayer ended, a beautiful bold-faced girl advanced to an open space in front of the altar, and with a sudden movement threw off her white robe, revealing herself to the spectators in a many-coloured garment of gauze, through which her fair flesh gleamed.

The black hair of this woman was adorned with a coronet of scarlet flowers and hung loose about her; her feet and arms were naked, and in each hand she held a knife of bronze. Very slowly she began to dance, her painted lips parted as though to speak, and her eyes, brightened with pigments, turned up to heaven. By degrees her movements grew more rapid, till at length, as she whirled round, her long locks streamed out straight upon the air and the crown of flowers looked like a scarlet ring. Suddenly the bronze knife in her right hand flashed, and a spot of red appeared above her left breast; then the knife in the left hand flashed, and another spot appeared over the right breast. At each stroke the multitude cried, "Ah!" as with one voice, and then were silent.

Now the maddened dancer, ceasing her whirlings, leapt high into the air, clashing the knives above her head and crying, "Hear me, hear me, Baaltis!"

Again she leapt, and this time the answer that came from her lips was spoken in another voice, which said, "I am present. What seek you?"

A third time the priestess leapt, replying in her own voice, "Health for thy servant who is sick." Then came the answer in the second voice —"I hear you, but I see no sacrifice."

"What sacrifice would'st thou, O Queen? A dove?"

"Nay."

"What then, Queen?"

"One only, the first-born child of a woman."

As this command, which they supposed to be divine and from above, issued out of the lips of the gashed and bleeding Pythoness, the multitude that hitherto had listened in perfect silence, shouted aloud, while the girl herself, utterly exhausted, fell to the earth swooning.

Now the high priest of El, who was named the Shadid, none other indeed than the husband of her who lay sick, sprang upon the platform and cried:—

"The goddess has spoken by the mouth of her oracle. She who is the mother of all demands one life out of the many she has given, that the Lady Baaltis, who is her priestess upon earth, may be recovered of her sickness. Say, who will lay down a life for the honour of the goddess, and that her regent in this land may be saved alive?"

Now—for all this scene had been carefully prepared—a woman stepped forward, wearing the robe of a priestess, who bore in her arms a drugged and sleeping child.

"I, father," she cried in a shrill, hard voice, though her lips trembled as she spoke. "Let the goddess take this child, the first- fruit of my body, that our mother the Lady Baaltis may be cured of her sickness, and that I, her daughter, may be blessed by the goddess, and through me, all we who worship her." And she held out the little victim towards him.

The Shadid stretched out his arms to take it, but he never did take it, for at that moment appeared upon the platform the tall and bearded figure of Issachar clad in his white robes.

"Hold!" he cried in a loud, clear voice, "and touch not the innocent child. Spawn of Satan, would you do murder to appease the devils whom you worship? Well shall they repay you, people of Zimboe. Oh! mine eyes are open and I see," he went on, shaking his thin arms above his head in a prophetic frenzy. "I see the sword of the true God, and it flames above this city of idolaters and abominations. I see this place of sacrifice, and I tell you that before the moon is young again it shall run red with the blood of you, idol worshippers, and of you, women of the groves. The heathen is at your gates, ye followers of demons, and my God sends them as He sends the locusts of the north wind to devour you like grass, to sweep you away like the dust of the desert. Cry then upon El and Baaltis, and let El and Baaltis save you if they can. Doom is upon you; Azrael, angel of death, writes his name upon your foreheads, every one of you, giving your city to the owls, your bodies to the jackals, and your souls to Satan—"

Thus far the priests and the spectators had listened to Issachar's denunciations in bewildered amazement not unmixed with fear. Now with a roar of wrath they awoke, and suddenly he was dragged from the platform by a score of hands and struck down with many blows. Indeed, he would then and there have been torn to pieces had not a guard of soldiers, knowing that he was Sakon's guest and in the train of the prince Aziel, snatched him from the maddened multitude, and borne him swiftly to a place of safety without the enclosure.

While the tumult was at its height, a Phoenician, who had arrived in the temple breathless with haste, might have been seen to pluck Metem by the sleeve.

"What is it?" Metem asked of the man, who was his servant.

"This: the lady Baaltis is dead. I watched as you bade me, and, as she had promised to do, in token of the end, her woman waved a napkin from the casement of that tower where she lies."

"Do any know of this?"

"None."

"Then say no word of it," and Metem hurried off in search of Aziel.

Presently he found him seeking for Issachar in company with his guards.

"Have no fear, Prince," Metem said, in answer to his eager questions, "he is safe enough, for the soldiers have borne the fool away. Pardon me that I should speak thus of a holy man, but he has put all our lives in danger."

"I do not pardon you," answered Aziel hotly, "and I honour Issachar for his act and words. Let us begone from this accursed place whither you entrapped me."

Before Metem could reply a voice cried, "Close the doors of the sanctuary, so that none can pass in or go out, and let the sacrifice be offered."

"Listen, Prince," said Metem, "you must stay here till the ceremony is done."

"Then I tell you, Phoenician," answered Aziel, "that rather than suffer that luckless child to be butchered before my eyes I will cut my way to it with my guards, and rescue it alive."

"To leave yourself dead in place of it," answered Metem sarcastically; "but, see, a woman desires to speak with you," and he pointed to a girl in the robe of a priestess, whose face was hidden with a veil, and who, in the tumult and confusion, had worked her way to Aziel.

"Prince," whispered the veiled form, "I am Elissa. For your life's sake keep still and silent, or you will be stabbed, for your words have been overheard, and the priests are mad at the insult that has been put upon them."

"Away with you, woman," answered Aziel; "what have I to do with a girl of the groves and a murderess of children?"

She winced at his bitter words, but said quietly:—

"Then on your own head be your blood, Prince, which I have risked much to keep unshed. But before you die, learn that I knew nothing of this foul sacrifice, and that gladly would I give my own life to save that of yonder child."

"Save it, and I will believe you," answered the prince, turning from her.

Elissa slipped away, for she saw that the priestesses, her companions, were reforming their ranks, and that she must not tarry. When she had gone a few yards, a hand caught her by the sleeve, and the voice of Metem, who had overheard something of this talk, whispered in her ear:—

"Daughter of Sakon, what will you give me if I show you a way to save the life of the child, and with it that of the prince, and at the same time to make him think well of you again?"

"All my jewels and ornaments of gold, and they are many," she answered eagerly.

"Good; it is a bargain. Now listen: The lady Baaltis is dead; she died a few minutes since, and none here know it save myself and one other, my servant, nor can any learn it, for the gates are shut. Do you be, therefore, suddenly inspired—of the gods—and say so, for then the sacrifice must cease, seeing that she for whom it was to be offered is dead. Do you understand?"

"I understand," she answered, "and though the blasphemy bring on me the vengeance of Baaltis, yet it shall be dared. Fear not, your pay is good," and she pressed forward to her place, keeping the veil wrapped about her head till she reached it unobserved, for in the general confusion none had noticed her movements.

When the noise of shouting and angry voices had at length died away, and the spectators were driven back outside the sacred circle, the priest upon the platform cried:—

"Now that the Jew blasphemer has gone, let the sacrifice be offered, as is decreed."

"Yea, let the sacrifice be offered," answered the multitude, and once more the woman with the sleeping child stepped forward. But before the priest could take it another figure approached him, that of Elissa, with arms outstretched and eyes upturned.

"Hold, O priest!" she said, "for the goddess, breathing on my brow, inspires me, and I have a message from the goddess."

"Draw near, daughter, and speak it in the ears of men," the priest answered wondering, for he found it hard to believe in such inspiration, and indeed would have denied her a hearing had he dared.

So Elissa climbed the platform, and standing upon it still with outstretched hands and upturned face, she said in a clear voice:—

"The goddess refuses the sacrifice, since she has taken to herself her for whom it was to have been offered—the Lady Baaltis is dead."

At this tidings a groan went up from the people, partly of grief for the loss of a spiritual dignitary who was popular, and partly of disappointment because now the sacrifice could not be offered. For the Phoenicians loved these horrible spectacles, which were not, however, commonly celebrated by daylight and in the presence of the people.

"It is a lie," cried a voice, "but now the Lady Baaltis was living."

"Let the gates be opened, and send to see whether or no I lie," said Elissa, quietly.

Then for a while there was silence while a priest went upon the errand. At length he was seen returning. Pushing his way through the crowd, he mounted the platform, and said:—

"The daughter of Sakon speaks truth; alas! the lady Baaltis is dead."

Elissa sighed in relief, for had her tidings proved false she could scarcely have hoped to escape the fury of the crowd.

"Ay!" she cried, "she is dead, as I told you, and because of your sin, who would have offered human sacrifice in public, against the custom of our faith and city and without the command of the goddess."

Then in sullen silence the priests and priestesses reformed their ranks, and departed from the sanctuary, whence they were followed by the spectators, the most of them in no good mood, for they had been baulked of the promised spectacle.

Chapter VI

The Hall of Audience

When Elissa reached her chamber after the break up of the procession, she threw herself upon her couch, and burst into a passion of tears. Well might she weep, for she had been false to her oath as a priestess, uttering as a message from the goddess that which she had learnt from the lips of man. More, she could not rid herself of the remembrance of the scorn and loathing with which the Prince Aziel had looked upon her, or of the bitter insult of his words when he called her, "a girl of the groves, and a murderess of children."

It chanced that, so far as Elissa was concerned, these charges were utterly untrue. None could throw a slur upon her, and as for these rare human sacrifices, she loathed the very name of them, nor, unless forced to it, would she have been present had she guessed that any such offering was intended.

Like most of the ancient religions, that of the Phoenicians had two sides to it—a spiritual and a material side. The spiritual side was a worship of the far-off unknown divinity, symbolised by the sun, moon and planets, and visible only in their majestic movements, and in the forces of nature. To this Elissa clung, knowing no truer god, and from those forces she strove to wring their secret, for her heart was deep. Lonely invocations to the goddess beneath the light of the moon appealed to her, for from them she seemed to draw strength and comfort, but the outward ceremonies of her faith, or the more secret and darker of them, of which in practice she knew little, were already an abomination in her eyes. And now what if the Jew prophet spoke truly? What if this creed of hers were a lie, root and branch, and there did lie in the heavens above a Lord and Father who heard and answered the prayers of men, and who did not seek of them the blood of the children He had given?

A great doubt took hold of Elissa and shook her being, and with the doubt came hope. How was it—if her faith were true—that when she took the name of the goddess in vain, nothing had befallen her? She desired to learn more of this matter, but who was to teach her? The Levite turned from her with loathing as from a thing unclean, and there remained, therefore, but the prince Aziel, who had put her from him with those bitter words of scorn. Ah! why did they pain her so, piercing her heart as with a spear? Was it because—because—he had grown dear to her? Yes, that was the truth. She had learned it even as he cursed her; all her quick southern blood was alight with a new fire, the like of which she had never known before. And not her blood only, it was her spirit—her spirit that yearned to his. Had it not leapt within her at the first sight of him as to one most dear, one long-lost and found again? She loved him, and he loathed her, and oh! her lot was hard.

As Elissa lay brooding thus in her pain, the door opened and Sakon, her father, hurried into the chamber.

"What is it that chanced yonder?" he asked, for he had not been present in the sanctuary, "and, daughter, why do you weep?"

"I weep, father, because your guest, the prince Aziel, has called me 'a girl of the groves, and a murderess of children,'" she replied.

"Then, by my head, prince that he is, he shall answer for it to me," said Sakon, grasping at his sword-hilt.

"Nay, father, since to him I must have seemed to deserve the words. Listen." And she told him all that had passed, hiding nothing.

"Now it seems that trouble is heaped upon trouble," said the Phoenician when she had finished, "and they were mad who suffered the prince and that fierce Issachar to be present at the sacrifice. Daughter, I tell you this: though I am a worshipper of El and Baaltis, as my fathers were before me, I know that Jehovah of the Jews is a great and powerful Lord, and that His prophets do not prophesy falsely, for I have seen it in my youth, yonder in the coasts of Sidon. What did Issachar say? That before the moon was young again, this temple should run red with blood? Well, so it may happen, for Ithobal threatens war against us, and for your sake, my daughter."

"How for my sake, father?" she asked heavily, as one who knew what the answer would be.

"You know well, girl. Ever since you danced before him at the great welcoming feast I made in his honour a month ago the man is besotted of you; moreover, he is mad with jealousy of this new-comer, the prince Aziel. He has demanded public audience of me this afternoon, and I have it privately that then he will formally ask you in marriage before the people, and if he is refused will declare war upon the city, with which he has many an ancient quarrel. Yes, yes, king Ithobal is that sword of God which the Jew said he saw hanging over us, and should it fall it will be because of you, Elissa."

"The Jew did not say that, father; he said it would be because of the sins of the people and their idolatries."

"What does it matter what he said?" broke in Sakon hastily. "How shall I answer Ithobal?"

"Tell him," she replied with a strange smile, "that he does wisely to be jealous of the prince Aziel."

"What! Of the stranger who this very day reviled you in words of such shame, and so soon?" asked her father astonished.

Elissa did not speak in answer; she only looked straight before her, and nodded her head.

"Had ever man such a daughter?" Sakon went on in petulant dismay. "Truly it is a wise saying which tells that women love those best who beat them, be it with the tongue or with the fist. Not but what I would gladly see you wedded to a prince of Israel and of Egypt rather than of this half-bred barbarian, but the legions of Solomon and of Pharaoh are far away, whereas Ithobal has a hundred thousand spears almost at our gate."

"There is no need to speak of such things, father," she said, turning aside, "since, even were I willing, the prince would have nought to do with me, who am a priestess of Baaltis."

"The matter of religion might be overcome," suggested Sakon; "but, no, for many reasons it is impossible. Well, this being so, daughter, I may answer Ithobal that you will wed him."

"I!" she said; "I wed that black-hearted savage? My father, you may answer what you will, but of this be sure, that I will go to my grave before I pass as wife to the board of Ithobal."

"Oh! my daughter," pleaded Sakon, "think before you say it. As his wife at least you, who are not of royal blood, will be a queen, and the mother of kings. But if you refuse, then either I must force you, which is hateful to me, or there will be such a war as the city has not known for generations, for Ithobal and his tribes have many grievances against us. By the gift of yourself, for a while, at any rate, you can, as it chances, make peace between us, but if that is withheld, then blood will run in rivers, and perhaps this city, with all who live in it, will be destroyed, or at the least its trade must be ruined and its wealth stolen away."

"If it is decreed that all these things are to be, they will be," answered Elissa calmly, "seeing that this war has threatened us for many years, and that a woman must think of herself first, and of the fate of cities afterwards. Of my own free will I shall never take Ithobal for husband. Father, I have said."

"Of the fate of cities, yes; but how of my fate, and that of those we love? Are we all to be ruined, and perhaps slaughtered, to satisfy your whim, girl?"

"I did not say so, father. I said that of my own free will I would not wed Ithobal. If you choose to give me to him you have the right to do it, but know then that you give me to my death. Perhaps it is best that it should be thus."

Sakon knew his daughter well, and it did not need that he should glance at her face to learn that she meant her words. Also he loved her, his only child, more dearly than anything on earth.

"In truth my strait is hard, and I know not which way to turn," he said, covering his face with his hand.

"Father," she replied, laying her fingers lightly on his shoulder, "what need is there to answer him at once? Take a month, or if he will not give it, a week. Much may happen in that time."

"The counsel is wise," he said, catching at this straw. "Daughter, be in the great hall of audience with your attendants three hours after noon, for then we must receive Ithobal boldly in all pomp, and deal with him as best we may. And now I go to ask peace for the Levite from the priests of El, and to discover whom the sacred colleges desire to nominate as the new Baaltis. Doubtless it will be Mesa, the daughter of her who is dead, though many are against her. Oh! if there were no priests and no women, this city would be easier to govern," and with an impatient gesture Sakon left the room.

It was three o'clock in the afternoon, and the great hall of audience in Zimboe was crowded with a brilliant assemblage. There sat Sakon, the governor, and with him his council of the notables of the city; there were prince Aziel and among his retinue, Issachar the prophet, fierce-eyed as ever, though hardly recovered from the rough handling he had experienced in the temple. There were representatives of the college of the priests of El. There were many ladies, wives and daughters of dignitaries and wealthy citizens, and with them a great crowd of spectators of all classes gathered in the lower part of the hall, for a rumour had spread about that the farewell audience given by Sakon to King Ithobal was likely to be stormy.

When all were gathered, a herald announced that Ithobal, King of the Tribes, waited to take his leave of Sakon, Governor of Zimboe, before departing to his own land on the morrow.

"Let him be admitted," said Sakon, who looked weary and ill at ease. Then as the herald bowed and left, he turned and whispered something into the ear of his daughter Elissa, who stood behind his chair, her face immovable as that of an Egyptian Sphinx, but magnificently apparelled in gleaming robes and jewelled ornaments—which Metem, looking on them, reflected with satisfaction were now his property.

Presently, preceded by a burst of savage music, Ithobal entered. He was gorgeously arrayed in a purple Tyrian robe decked with golden chains, while on the brow, in token of his royalty, he wore a golden circlet in which was set a single blood-red stone. Before him walked a sword-bearer carrying a sword of ceremony, a magnificent ivory-handled weapon encrusted with rough gems and inlaid with gold, while behind him, clad in barbaric pomp, marched a number of counsellors and attendants, huge and half-savage men who glared wonderingly at the splendour of the place and its occupants. As the king came, Sakon rose from his chair of state and, advancing down the hall, took him by the hand and led him to a similar chair placed at a little distance.

Ithobal seated himself and looked around the hall. Presently his glance fell upon Aziel, and he scowled.

"Is it common, Sakon," he asked, "that the seat of a prince should be set higher than that of a crowned king?" And he pointed to the chair of Aziel, which was placed a little above his own upon the daïs.

The governor was about to answer when Aziel said coldly:—

"Where it was pointed out to me that I should sit, there I sat, though, for aught I care, the king Ithobal may take my place. The grandson of Pharaoh and of Solomon does not need to dispute for precedence with the savage ruler of savage tribes."

Ithobal sprang to his feet and cried, grasping his sword:—

"By my father's soul, you shall answer for this, Princelet."

"You should have sworn by your mother's soul, King Ithobal," replied Aziel quietly, "for doubtless it is the black blood in your veins that causes you to forget your courtesy. For the rest, I answer to no man save to my king."

"Yet there is one other who will make you answer," replied Ithobal, in a voice thick with rage, "and here he is," and he drew his sword and flashed it before the prince's eyes. "Or if you fear to face him, then the wands of my slaves shall cause you to cry me pardon."

"If you desire to challenge me to combat, king Ithobal, for this purpose only I am your servant, though the fashion of your challenging is not that of any nation which I know."

Before Ithobal could reply, Sakon cried out in a loud voice:—

"Enough, enough! Is this a place for brawling, king Ithobal, and would you seek to fix a quarrel upon my guest, the prince Aziel, here in my council chamber, and to bring upon me the wrath of Israel, of Tyre, and of Egypt? Be sure that the prince shall cross no swords with you; no, not if I have to set him under guard to keep him safe. To your business, king Ithobal, or I break up this assembly and send you under escort to our gates."

Now his counsellors plucked Ithobal by the sleeve and whispered to him some advice, which at last he seemed to take with an ill grace, for, turning, he said, "So be it. This is my business, Sakon: For many years I and the countless tribes whom I rule have suffered much at the hands of you Phoenicians, who centuries ago settled here in my country as traders. That you should trade we are content, but not that you should establish yourselves as a sovereign power, pretending to be my equals who are my servants. Therefore, in the name of my nation, I demand that the tribute which you pay to me for the use of the mines of gold shall henceforth be doubled; that the defences of this city be thrown down; and that you cease to enslave the natives of the land to labour in your service. I have spoken."

Now as these arrogant demands reached their ears, the company assembled in the hall murmured with anger and astonishment, then turned to wait for Sakon's answer.

"And if we refuse these small requests of yours, O King?" asked the governor sarcastically, "what then? Will you make war upon us?"

"First tell me, Sakon, if you do refuse them?"

"In the name of the cities of Tyre and Sidon whom I serve, and of Hiram my master, I refuse them one and all," answered Sakon with dignity.

"Then, Sakon, I am minded to bring up a hundred thousand men against you and to sweep you and your city from the face of earth," said Ithobal. "Yet I remember that I also have Phoenician blood in my veins mixed with the nobler and more ancient blood at which yonder upstart jeers, and therefore I would spare you. I remember also that for generations there has been peace and amity between my forefathers and the Council of this city, and therefore I would spare you. Behold, then, I build a bridge whereby you may escape, asking but one little thing of you in proof that you are indeed my friend, and it is that you give me your daughter, the lady Elissa, whom I seek to make my queen. Think well before you answer, remembering that upon this answer may hang the lives of all who listen to you, ay, and of many thousand others."

For a while there was silence in the assemblage, and every eye was fixed upon Elissa, who stood neither moving nor speaking, her face still set like that of a Sphinx, and almost as unreadable. Aziel gazed at her with the rest, and his eyes she felt alone of all the hundreds that were bent upon her. Indeed, so strongly did they draw her, that against her own will she turned her head and met them. Then remembering what had passed between herself and the prince that very day, she coloured faintly and looked down, neither the glance nor the blush escaping the watchful Ithobal.

Presently Sakon spoke:—

"King Ithobal," he said, "I am honoured indeed that you should seek my daughter as your queen, but she is my only child, whom I love, and I have sworn to her that I will not force her to marry against her will, whoever be the suitor. Therefore, King, take your answer from her own lips, for whatever it be it is my answer."

"Lady," said Ithobal, "you have heard your father's words; be pleased to say that you look with favour upon my suit, and that you will deign to share my throne and power."

Elissa took a step forward on the daïs and curtseyed low before the king.

"O King!" she said, "I am your handmaid, and great indeed is the favour that you would do your servant. Yet, King, I Pray of you search out some fairer woman of a more royal rank to share your crown and sceptre, for I am all unworthy of them, and to those words on this matter which I have spoken in past days I have none to add." Then again she curtseyed, adding, "King, I am your servant."

Now a murmur of astonishment went up from the audience, for few of them thought it possible that Elissa, who, however beautiful, was but the daughter of a noble, could refuse to become the wife of a king. Ithobal alone did not seem to be astonished, for he had expected this answer.

"Lady," he said, repressing with an effort the passions which were surging within him, "I think that I have something to offer to the woman of my choice, and yet you put me aside as lightly as though I had neither name, nor power, nor station. This, as it seems to me, can be read in one way only, that your heart is given elsewhere."

"Have it as you will, King," answered Elissa, "my heart is given elsewhere."

"And yet, lady, not four suns gone you swore to me that you loved no man. Since then it seems that you have learned to love, and swiftly, and it is yonder Jew whom you have chosen." And he pointed to the prince Aziel.

Again Elissa coloured, this time to the eyes, but she showed no other sign of confusion.

"May the king pardon me," she said, "and may the prince Aziel, whose name has thus been coupled with mine, pardon me. I said indeed that my heart was given elsewhere, but I did not say it was given to any man. May not the heart of a mortal maid-priestess be given to the Ever- living?"

Now for a moment the king was silenced, while a murmur of applause at her ready wit went round the audience. But before it died away a voice at the far end of the hall called out:—

"Perchance the lady does not know that yonder in Egypt, and in Jerusalem also, prince Aziel is named the Ever-living."

Now it was Elissa's turn to be overcome.

"Nay, I knew it not," she said; "how should I know it? I spoke of that Dweller in the heavens whom I worship—"

"And behold, the title fits a dweller on the earth whom you must also worship, for such omens do not come by chance," cried the same voice, but from another quarter of the crowded hall.

"I ask pardon," broke in Aziel, "and leave to speak. It is true that owing to a certain birth-mark which I bear, among the Egyptians I have been given the bye-name of the Ever-living, but it is one which this lady can scarcely have heard, therefore jest no more upon a chance accident of words. Moreover, if you be men, cease to heap insult upon a woman. I who am almost a stranger here have not dared to ask the lady Elissa for her favour."

"Ay, but you will ask and she will grant," answered the same voice, the owner of which none could discover—for he seemed to speak from every part of the chamber.

"Indeed," went on Aziel, not heeding the interruption, "the last words between us were words of anger, for we quarrelled on a matter of religion."

"What of that?" cried the voice; "love is the highest of religions, for do not the Phoenicians worship it?"

"Seize yonder knave," shouted Sakon, and search was made but without avail. Afterwards, however, Aziel remembered that once, when they were weather-bound on their journey from the coast, Metem had amused them by making his voice sound from various quarters of the hut in which they lay. Then Ithobal rose and said:—

"Enough of this folly; I am not here to juggle with words, or to listen to such play. Whether the lady Elissa spoke of the gods she serves or of a man is one to me. I care not of whom she spoke, but for her words I do care. Now hearken, you city of traders: If this is to be thy answer, then I break down that bridge which I have built, and it is war between you and my Tribes, war to the end. But let her change her words, and whether she loves me or loves me not, come to be my wife, and, for my day, the bridge shall stand; for once that we are wed I can surely teach her love, or if I cannot, at least it is she I seek with or without her love. Reflect then, lady, and reply again, remembering how much hangs upon your lips."

"Do you think, king Ithobal," Elissa answered, looking at him with angry eyes, "that a woman such as I am can be won by threats? I have spoken, king Ithobal."

"I know not," he replied; "but I do know that she can be won by force, and then surely, lady, your pride shall pay the price, for you shall be mine, but not my queen."

Now one of the council rose and said:—

"It seems, Sakon, that there is more in this matter than whether or no the king Ithobal pleases your daughter. Is the city then to be plunged into a great war, of which none can see the end, because one woman looks askance upon a man? Better that a thousand girls should be wedded where they would not than that such a thing should happen. Sakon, according to our ancient law you have the right to give your daughter in marriage where and when you will. We demand, therefore, that for the good of the commonwealth, you should exercise this right, and hand over the lady Elissa to king Ithobal."

This speech was received with loud and general shouts of approval, for no Phoenician audience would have been willing to sacrifice its interests for a thing so trivial as the happiness of a woman.

"Between the desire of a beloved daughter to whom I have pledged my word and my duty to the great city over which I rule, my strait is hard indeed," answered Sakon. "Hearken, king Ithobal, I must have time. Give me eight days from now in which to answer you, for if you will not, I deny your suit."

Ithobal seemed about to refuse the demand of Sakon. Then once more his counsellors plucked him by the sleeve, pointing out to him that if he did this, it was likely that none of them would leave the city alive. At some sign from the governor, they whispered, the captains of the guard were already hastening from the hall.

"So be it, Sakon," he said. "To-night I camp without your walls, which are no longer safe for one who has threatened war against them, and on the eighth day from this see to it that your heralds being me the Lady Elissa and peace—or I make good my threat. Till then, farewell." And placing himself in the midst of his company king Ithobal left the hall.

Chapter VII

The Black Dwarf

Some two hours had passed since the break-up of the assembly in the great hall. Prince Aziel was seated in his chamber, when the keeper of the door announced that a woman was without who desired to speak with him. He gave orders that she should be admitted, and presently a veiled figure entered the room and bowed before him.

"Be pleased to unveil, and to tell me your business," he said.

With some reluctance his visitor withdrew the wrapping from her head, revealing a face which Aziel recognised as one that he had seen among the waiting women who attended on Elissa.

"My message is for your ear, Prince," she said, glancing at the man who had ushered her into the chamber.

"It is not my custom to receive strangers thus alone," said the prince; "but be it as you will," and he motioned to the servant to retire without the door. "I await your pleasure," he added, when the man had gone.

"It is here," she answered, and drew from her bosom a little papyrus roll.

"Who wrote this?" he asked.

"I know not, Prince; it was given to me to pass on to you."

Then he opened the roll and read. It ran thus: "Though we parted with bitter words, still in my sore distress I crave the comfort of your counsel. Therefore, since I am forbidden to speak with you openly, meet me, I beseech you, at moonrise in the palace garden under the shade of the great fig tree with five roots, where I shall be accompanied only by one I trust. Bring no man with you for my safety's sake.—Elissa."

Aziel thrust the scroll into his robe, and thought awhile. Then he gave the waiting lady a piece of gold and said:—

"Tell her who sent you that I obey her words. Farewell."

This message seemed to puzzle the woman, who opened her lips to speak. Then, changing her mind, she turned and went.

Scarcely had she gone when the Phoenician, Metem, was ushered into the room.

"O Prince," he said maliciously, "pardon me if I caution you. Yet in truth if veiled ladies flit thus through your apartments in the light of day, it will reach the ears of the holy but violent Issachar, of whose doings I come to speak. Then, Prince, I tremble for you."

Aziel made a movement half-impatient and half-contemptuous. "The woman is a serving-maid," he said, "who brought me a message that I understand but little. Tell me, Metem, for you know this place of old, does there stand in the palace garden a great fig tree with five roots?"

"Yes, Prince; at least such a tree used to grow there when last I visited this country. It was one of the wonders of the town, because of its size. What of it?"

"Little, except that I must be under it at moonrise. See and read, since whatever you may say of yourself, you are, I think, no traitor."

"Not if I am well paid to keep counsel, Prince," Metem answered with a smile. Then he read the scroll.

"I am glad that the noble lady brings an attendant with her," he said as he returned it, with a bow. "The gossips of Zimboe are censorious, and might misinterpret this moonlight meeting, as indeed would Sakon and Issachar. Well, doves will coo and maids will woo, and unless I can make money out of it the affair is none of mine."

"Have I not told you that there is no question of wooing?" asked the prince angrily. "I go only to give her what counsel I can in the matter of the suit of this savage, Ithobal. The lady Elissa and I have quarrelled beyond repair over that accursed sacrifice—"

"Which her ready wit prevented," put in Metem.

"But I promised last night that I would help her if I could," the prince went on, "and I always keep my word."

"I understand, Prince. Well, since you turn from the lady, whose name with yours is so much in men's mouths just now, doubtless you will give her wise counsel, namely, to wed Ithobal, and lift the shadow of war from this city. Then, indeed, we shall all be grateful to you, for it seems that no one else can move her stubbornness. And, by the way: If, when she has listened to your wisdom, the daughter of Sakon should chance to explain to you that the sight of this day's attempted sacrifice filled her with horror, and that she parted with every jewel she owns to put an end to it—well, her words will be true. But, since you have quarrelled, they will have no more interest for you, Prince, than has my talk about them. So now to other matters." And Metem began to speak of the conduct of Issachar in the sanctuary, and of the necessity of guarding him against assassination at the hands of the priests of El as a consequence of his religious zeal. Presently he was gone, leaving Aziel somewhat bewildered.

Could it be true, as she herself had told him, and as Metem now asserted, that Elissa had not participated willingly in the dark rites in the temple? If so he had misjudged her and been unjust; indeed, what atonement could suffice for such words as he had used towards her? Well, to some extent she must have understood and forgiven them, otherwise she would scarcely have sought his aid, though he knew not how he could help her in her distress.

When Elissa returned from the assembly, she laid herself down to rest, worn out in mind and body. Soon sleep came to her, and with the sleep dreams. At first these were vague and shadowy, then they grew more clear. She dreamed that she saw a dim and moonlit garden, and in it a vast tree with twisted roots that seemed familiar to her. Something moving among the branches of this tree attracted her attention, but for a long while she watched it without being able to discover what it was. Now she saw. The moving thing was a hideous black dwarf with beady eyes, who held in his hand a little ivory tipped bow, on the string of which was set an arrow. Her consciousness concentrated itself upon this arrow, and though she knew not how, she became aware that it was poisoned. What was the dwarf doing in the tree with a bow and poisoned arrow, she wondered? Suddenly a sound seemed to strike her ear, the sound of a man's footsteps walking over grass, and she perceived that the figure of the dwarf, crouched upon the bough, became tense and alert, and that his fingers tightened upon the bow- string until the blood was driven from their yellow tips. Following the glance of his wicked black eyes, she saw advancing through the shadow a tall man clad in a dark robe. Now he emerged into a patch of moonlight and stood looking around him as though he were searching for some one. Then the dwarf raised himself to his knees upon the bough, and, aiming at the bare throat of the man, drew the bow-string to his ear. At this moment the victim turned his head and the moonlight shone full upon his face. It was that of the prince Aziel.

Elissa awoke from her vision with a little cry, then rose trembling, and strove to comfort herself in the thought that although it was so very vivid she had dreamed but a dream. Still shaken and unnerved, she passed into another chamber, and made pretence to eat of the meal that was made ready for her, for it was now the hour of sunset. While she was thus employed, it was announced that the Phoenician, Metem, desired to speak with her, and she commanded that he should be admitted.

"Lady," he said bowing, so soon as her attendants had withdrawn to the farther end of the chamber, "you can guess my errand. This morning I gave you certain tidings which proved both true and useful, and for those tidings you promised a reward."

"It is so," she said, and going to a chest she drew from it an ivory casket full of ornaments of gold and among them necklaces and other objects set with uncut precious stones. "Take them," she said, "they are yours; that is, save this gold chain alone, for it is vowed to Baaltis."

"But lady," he asked, "how can you appear before Ithobal the king thus robbed of all your ornaments?"

"I shall not appear before Ithobal the king," she answered sharply.

"You say so! Then what will the prince Aziel think of you when he sees you thus unadorned?"

"My beauty is my adornment," she replied, "not these gems and gold. Moreover, it is nought to me what he thinks, for he hates me, and has reviled me."

Metem lifted his eyebrows incredulously and went on: "Still, I will not deprive you of this woman's gear. Look now, I value it, and at no high figure," and drawing out his writer's palette and a slip of papyrus, he wrote upon it an acknowledgment of debt, which he asked her to sign.

"This document, lady," he said, "I will present to your father—or your husband—at a convenient season, nor do I fear that either of them will refuse to honour it. And now I take my leave, for you—have an appointment to keep—and," he added with emphasis, "the time of moonrise is at hand."

"Your meaning, I pray you?" she asked. "I have no appointment at moonrise, or at any other hour."

Metem bowed politely, but in a fashion which showed that he put no faith in her words.

"Again I ask your meaning, merchant," she said, "for your dark hintings are scarcely to be borne."

The Phoenician looked at her; there was a ring of truth in her voice.

"Lady," he said, "will you indeed deny, after I have seen it written by yourself, that within some few minutes you meet the prince Aziel beneath a great tree in the palace gardens, there—so said the scroll —to ask his aid in this matter of the suit of Ithobal?"

"Written by myself?" she said wonderingly. "Meet the prince Aziel beneath a tree in the palace gardens? Never have I thought of it."

"Yet, lady, the scroll I saw purported to be written by you, and your own woman bore it to the prince. As I think, she sits yonder at the end of the chamber, for I know her shape."

"Come hither," called Elissa, addressing the woman. "Now tell me, what scroll was this that you carried to-day to the prince Aziel, saying that I sent you?"

"Lady," answered the girl confusedly, "I never told the prince Aziel that you sent him the scroll."

"The truth, woman, the truth," said her mistress. "Lie not, or it will be the worse for you."

"Lady, this is the truth. As I was walking through the market-place an old black woman met me, and offered me a piece of gold if I would deliver a letter into the hand of the prince Aziel. The gold tempted me, for I had need of it, and I consented; but of who wrote the letter I know nothing, nor have I ever seen the woman before."

"You have done wrong, girl," said Elissa, "but I believe your tale. Now go."

When she had gone, Elissa stood for a while thinking; and, as she thought, Metem saw a look of fear gather on her face.

"Say," she asked him, "is there anything strange about the tree of which the scroll tells?"

"Its size is strange," he answered, "and it has five roots that stand above the ground."

As he spoke Elissa uttered a little cry.

"Ah!" she said, "it is the tree of my dream. Now—now I understand. Swift, oh! come with me swiftly, for see, the moon rises," and she sprang to the door followed by the amazed Metem.

Another minute, and they were speeding down the narrow street so fast that those who loitered there turned their heads and laughed, for they thought that a jealous husband pursued his wife. As Elissa fumbled at the hasp of the door of the garden, Metem overtook her.

"What means this hunt?" he gasped.

"That they have decoyed the prince here to murder him," she answered, and sped through the gateway.

"Therefore we must be murdered also. A woman's logic," the Phoenician reflected to himself as he panted after her.

Swiftly as Elissa had run down the street, here she redoubled her speed, flitting through the glades like some white spirit, and so rapidly that her companion found it difficult to keep her in view. At length they came to a large open space of ground where played the level beams of the rising moon, striking upon the dense green foliage of an immense tree that grew there. Round this tree Elissa ran, glancing about her wildly, so that for a few seconds Metem lost sight of her, for its mass was between them. When he saw her again she was speeding towards the figure of a man who stood in the open, about ten paces from the outer boughs of the tree. To this she pointed as she came, crying out aloud, "Beware! Beware!"

Another moment and she had almost reached the man, and still pointing began to gasp some broken words. Then, suddenly in the bright moonlight, Metem saw a shining point of light flash towards the pair from the darkness of the tree. It would seem that Elissa saw it also; at least, she leapt from the ground, her arm lifted above her head as though to catch the object. Then as her feet once more touched the earth her knees gave way, and she fell down with a moan of pain. Metem running on towards her, as he went perceived a shape, which looked like that of a black dwarf, slip from the shadow of the tree into some bushes beyond where it was lost. Now he was there, to find Elissa half-seated, half-lying on the ground, the prince Aziel bending over her, and fixed through the palm of her right hand, which she held up piteously, a little ivory-pointed arrow.

"Draw it out from the wound," he panted.

"It will not help me," she answered; "the arrow is poisoned."

With an exclamation, Metem knelt beside her, and, not heeding her groans of pain, drew the dart through the pierced palm. Then he tore a strip of linen from his robe, and knotting it round Elissa's wrist, he took a broken stick that lay near and twisted the linen till it almost cut into her flesh.

"Now, Prince," he said, "suck the wound, for I have no breath for it. Fear not, lady, I know an antidote for this arrow poison, and presently I will be back with the salve. Till then, if you would live, do not suffer that bandage to be loosed, however much it pains you," and he departed swiftly.

Aziel put his lips to the hurt to draw out the poison.

"Nay," she said faintly, trying to pull away her hand, "it is not fitting, the venom may kill you."

"It seems that it was meant for me," he answered, "so at the worst I do take but my own."

Presently, directing Elissa to hold her hand above her head, he put his arms about her and carried her a hundred paces or more into the open glade.

"Why do you move me?" she asked, her head resting on his shoulder.

"Because whoever it was that shot the arrow may return to try his fortune a second time, and here in the open his darts cannot reach us." Then he set her down upon the grass and stood looking at her.

"Listen, prince Aziel," Elissa said after a while, "the venom with which these black men soak their weapons is very strong, and unless Metem's salve be good, it may well chance that I shall die. Therefore before I die I wish to say a word to you. What brought you to this place to-night?"

"A letter from yourself, lady."

"I know it," she said, "but I did not write that letter; it was a snare, set, as I think, by the king Ithobal, who would do you to death in this way or in that. A messenger of his bribed my waiting-maid to deliver it, and afterwards I learnt the tale from Metem. Then, guessing all, I came hither to try to save you."

"But how could you guess all, lady?"

"In a strange fashion, Prince." And in a few words she told him her dream.

"This is marvellous indeed, that you should be warned of my danger by visions," he said wondering, and half-doubtingly.

"So marvellous, Prince, that you do not believe me," Elissa answered. "I know well what you think. You think that a woman to whom this very morning you spoke such words as women cannot well forgive, being revengeful laid a plot to murder you, and then, being a woman, changed her mind. Well, it is not so; Metem can prove it to you!"

"Lady, I believe you," he said, "without needing the testimony of Metem. But now the story grows still more strange, for if you had done me no wrong, how comes it that to preserve me from harm you set your tender flesh between the arrow and one who had reviled you?"

"It was by chance," she answered faintly. "I learnt the truth and ran to warn you. Then I saw the arrow fly towards your heart, and strove to grasp it, and it pierced me. It was by chance, by such a chance as made me dream your danger." And she fainted.

Chapter VIII

Aziel Plights His Troth

At first Aziel feared that the poison had done its work, and that Elissa was dead, till placing his hand upon her heart he felt it beating faintly, and knew that she did but swoon. To leave her to seek water or assistance was impossible, since he dared not loose his hold of the bandage about her wrist. So, patiently as he might, he knelt at her side awaiting the return of Metem.

How beautiful her pale face seemed there in the moonlight, set in its frame of dusky hair. And how strange was this tale of hers, of a dream that she had dreamed, a dream which, to save his own, led her to offer her life to the murderer's arrow. Many would not believe it, but he felt that it was true; he felt that even if she wished it she could not lie to him, for as he had known since first they met, their souls were open to each other. Yes, having thus been warned of his danger, she had offered her life for him—for him who that morning had called her, unjustly so Metem said, "a girl of the groves and a murderess." How came it that she had done this, unless indeed she loved him as—he loved her?

Aziel could no longer palter with himself, it was the truth. Last night when Issachar accused him, he had felt this, although then he would not admit it altogether, and now to-night he knew that his fate had found him. They would say that, after the common fashion of men, he had been conquered by a lovely face and form and a brave deed of devotion. But it was not so. Something beyond the flesh and its works and attributes drew him towards this woman, something that he could neither understand nor define (unless, indeed, the vision of Issachar defined it), but of which he had been conscious since first he set eyes upon her face. It was possible, it was even probable, that before another hour had gone by she would have passed beyond his reach, into the deeps of death, whither for a while he could not follow her. Yet he knew that the knowledge that she never could be his would not affect the love of her which burnt in him, for his desire towards her was not altogether a desire of the earth.

Aziel bent down over the swooning girl, looking into her pale face, till her lips almost touched his own, and his breath beating on her brow seemed to give her life again. Now she stirred, and now she opened her eyes and gazed back at him a while, deeply and with meaning, even as he gazed at her.

He spoke no word, for his lips seemed to be smitten with silence, but his heart said, "I love you, I love you," and her heart heard it, for she whispered back:—

"Bethink you who and what I am."

"It matters not, for we are one," he replied.

"Bethink you," she said again, "that soon I may be dead and lost to you."

"It cannot be, for we are one," he replied. "One we have been, one we are to-day, and one we shall be through all the length of life and death."

"Prince," she said again, "once more and for the last time I say: Bethink you well, for it comes upon me that your words are true, and that if I take that which to-night you offer, it will be for ever and for aye."

"For ever and aye, let it be," Aziel said, leaning towards her.

"For ever and for aye, let it be," she repeated, holding up her lips to his.

And thus in the silent moonlit garden they plighted their strange troth.

"Lady," said a voice in their ears, the voice of Metem, "I pray you let me dress your hand, for there is no time to lose."

Aziel looked up to see the Phoenician bending over them with a sardonic smile, and behind him the tall form of Issachar, who stood regarding them, his arms folded on his breast.

"Holy Issachar," went on Metem with malice, "be pleased to hold this lady's hand, since it seems that the prince here can only tend her lips."

"Nay," answered the Levite, "what have I to do with this daughter of Baaltis? Cure her if you can, or if you cannot, let her die, for so shall a stone of stumbling be removed from the feet of the foolish." And he glanced indignantly at Aziel.

"Had it not been for this same stone at least the feet of the foolish by now would have pointed skywards. The gods send me such a stone if ever a black dwarf draws a poisoned arrow at me," answered Metem, as he busied himself with his drugs. Then he added, "Nay, Prince, do not stop to answer him, but hold the lady's hand to the light."

Aziel obeyed, and having washed out the wound with water, Metem rubbed ointment into it which burnt Elissa so sorely that she groaned aloud.

"Be patient beneath the pain, lady," he said, "for if it has not already passed into your blood, this salve will eat away the poison of the arrow."

Then half-leading and half-carrying her, they brought her back to the palace. Here Metem gave her over into the care of her father, telling him as much of the story as he thought wise, and cautioning him to keep silent concerning what had happened.

At the door of the palace Issachar spoke to Aziel.

"Did I dream, Prince," he said, "or did my ears indeed hear you tell that idolatress that you loved her for ever, and did my eyes see you kiss her on the lips?"

"It seems that you saw and heard these things, Issachar," said Aziel, setting his face sternly. "Now hear this further, and then I pray you give me peace on this matter of the lady Elissa: If in any way it is possible, I shall make her my wife, and if it be not possible, then for so long as she may live at least I will look upon no other woman."

"Then that is good news, Prince, to me, who am charged with your welfare, for be sure, if I can prevent you, you shall never mix your life with that of this heathen sorceress."

"Issachar," the prince replied, "I have borne much from you because I know well that you love me, and have stood to me in the place of a father. But now, in my turn, I warn you, do not seek to work harm to the lady Elissa, for in striking her you strike me, and such blows may bring my vengeance after them."

"Vengeance?" mocked the Levite. "I fear but one vengeance, and it is not yours, nor do I listen to the whisperings of love when duty points the path. Rather would I see you dead, prince Aziel, then lured down to hell by the wiles of yonder witch."

Then before Aziel could answer he turned and left him.

As Issachar went to his own chamber full of bitterness and indignation, he passed the door of Elissa's apartments, and came face to face with Metem issuing from them.

"Will the woman live?" he asked of him.

"Be comforted, worthy Issachar. I think so; that is, if the bandage does not slip. I go to tell the prince."

"Gladly would I give a hundred golden shekels to him who brought me tidings that it had slipped and the woman with it, down to the arms of her father Beelzebub," broke in the Levite passionately.

"Pretty words for a holy man," said Metem, feigning amazement. "Well, Issachar, I will do most things for good money, but to shift that bandage would be but murder, and this I cannot work even for the gold and to win your favour."

"Fool," answered Issachar, "did I ask you to do murder? I do not fight with such weapons; let the woman live or die as it is decreed. Nay, enter my chamber, for I would speak with you, who are a cunning man versed in the craft of courts. Listen now: I love this prince Aziel, for I have reared him from his childhood, and he has been a son to me who have none. More, I am sent hither to this hateful land to watch him and hold him from harm, and for all that chances to him I must account. And now, what has chanced? This woman, Elissa, by her witcheries—"

"Softly, Issachar; what witcheries does she need beyond those lips and form and eyes?"

"By her witcheries, I tell you, has ensnared him so that now he swears that he will wed her."

"What of it, Issachar? He might travel far to find a lovelier woman."

"What of it, do you ask, remembering who he is? What of it, when you know his faith, and that this fair idolater will sap it, and cause him to cast away his soul? What of it, when with your own ears you heard him swear to love her through all the deeps of life and death? Man, are you mad?"

"No, but some might say that you are, holy father, who forget that I am also of this religion which you revile. But for good or ill, so the matter stands; and now what is it that you wish of me?"

"I wish that you should make it impossible that the prince Aziel should take this woman to wife. Not by murder, indeed, for 'thou shalt not kill,' saith the law, but by bringing it about that she should marry the king Ithobal, or if that fail, in any other fashion which seems good to you."

"'Thou shalt not kill,' saith your law; tell me then, Issachar, does it say also that thou shalt hand over a woman to a fate that she chances to hold to be worse than death? Doubtless it is foolish of her, and we should not heed such woman's folly. Yet this one has a certain strength of will, and I question if all the elders of the city will bring her living to the arms of Ithobal."

"It is nought to me, Metem, if she weds Ithobal, or weds him not, save that I do not love this heathen man, and surely her temper and her witcheries would bring ruin on him. What I would have you do is to prevent her from marrying Aziel; the way I leave to you."

"And what should I be paid for this service, holy Issachar?"

The Jew thought and answered, "A hundred golden shekels."

"Two hundred gold shekels," replied Metem reflectively, "nay, I am sure you said two hundred, Issachar. At least, I do not work for less, and it is a small sum enough, seeing that to earn it I must take upon myself the guilt of severing two loving hearts. But I know well that you are right, and that this would be an evil marriage for the prince Aziel, and also for the lady Elissa, who then day by day and year by year must bear the scourge of your reproaches, Issachar. Therefore I will do my best, not for the money indeed, but because I see herein a righteous duty. And now here is parchment, give me the lamp that I may prepare the bond."

"My word is my bond, Phoenician," answered the Levite haughtily.

Metem looked at him. "Doubtless," he said, "but you are old, and this is—a rough country where accidents chance at times. Still, the thing would read very ill, and, as you say, your word is your bond. Only remember, Issachar, two hundred shekels, bearing interest at two shekels a month. And now you are weary, holy Issachar, with plotting for the welfare of others, and so am I. Farewell, and good dreams to you."

The Levite watched him go, muttering to himself, "Alas that I should have fallen to such traffic with a knave, but it is for your sake and for your soul's sake, O Aziel my son. I pray that Fate be not too strong for me and you."

For two days from this night Elissa lay almost senseless, and by many it was thought that she would die. But when Metem saw her on the morning after she had been wounded, and noted that her arm was but little swollen, and had not turned black, he announced that she would certainly live, whatever the doctors of the city might declare. Thereon Sakon, her father, and Aziel blessed him, but Issachar said nothing.

As the Phoenician was walking through the market-place early on the next day an aged black woman, whom he did not know, accosted him, saying that she had a message for his ear from the king Ithobal who was camped without the city and who desired to see the merchandise that he had brought with him from the coasts of Tyre. Now Metem had already sold all his wares at a great advantage; still, as he would not neglect this opportunity of trade, he purchased others from his fellow merchants, and loading two camels with them, set out for the camp of Ithobal, riding on a mule. By midday he had reached it. The camp was pitched near water in a pleasant grove of trees, and on one of these not far from the tent of Ithobal Metem noted that there hung the body of a black dwarf.

"Behold the fate of him who shoots at the buck and hits the doe. Well, I have always said that murder is a dangerous game, since blood calls out for blood," thought Metem as he rode towards the tent.

At its door stood king Ithobal looking very huge and sullen in the sunlight. Metem dismounted and prostrated himself obsequiously.

"May the King live for ever," he said, "the great King, the King to whom all the other kings of the earth are as the little gods to Baal, or the faint stars to the sun."

"Rise, and cease from flatteries," said Ithobal shortly; "I may be greater than the other kings, but at least you do not think it."

"If the king says so, so let it be," replied Metem calmly. "A woman yonder in the market-place told me that the king wished to trade for my merchandise. So I have brought the best of it; priceless goods that which much toil I have carried hither from Tyre," and he pointed to the two camels laden with the inferior articles which he had purchased, and began to read the number and description of the goods from his tablets.

"What value do you set upon the whole of them, merchant?" asked Ithobal.

"To the traders of the country so much, but to you, O King, so much only," and he named a sum twice that which he had paid in the city.

"So be it," assented Ithobal indifferently; "I do not haggle over wares. Though your price is large, presently my treasurer shall weigh you out the gold."

There was a moment's pause, then Metem said:—

"The trees in this camp of yours bear evil fruit, O King. If I might ask, why does that little black monkey hang yonder."

"Because he tried to do murder with his poisoned arrows," answered Ithobal sullenly.

"And failed? Well, it must comfort you to think that he did fail if he was of the number of your servants. It is strange now that some knave unknown attempted murder last night in the palace gardens, also with poisoned arrows. I say attempted, but as yet I cannot be sure that he did not succeed."

"What!" exclaimed Ithobal, "was—" and he stopped.

"No, King, prince Aziel was not hit; the Lady Elissa took that shaft through her hand, and lies between life and death. I am doctoring her, and had it not been for my skill she would now be stiff and black—as the rogue who shot the arrow."

"Save her," said Ithobal hoarsely, "and I will pay you a doctor's fee of a hundred ounces of pure gold. Oh! had I but known, the clumsy fool should not have died so easily."

Metem took out his tablets and made a note of the amount.

"Take comfort, King," he said, "I think that I shall earn the fee. But to speak truth, this matter looks somewhat ugly, and your name is mentioned in it. Also it is said that your cousin, the great man whom the prince Aziel slew, was charged to abduct a certain lady by your order."

"Then false tales are told in Zimboe, and not for the first time," answered Ithobal coldly. "Listen, merchant, I have a question to ask of you. Will the prince Aziel meet me in single combat with whatever weapons he may choose?"

"Doubtless, and—pardon me if I say it—slay you as he slew your cousin, for he is a fine swordsman, who has studied the art in Egypt, where it is understood, and your strength would not avail against him. But your question is already answered, for though the prince would be glad enough to fight you, Sakon will have none of it. Have you nothing else to ask me, King?"

Ithobal nodded and said:—

"Listen, merchant. I know your repute of old, that you love money and will do much to gain it, and that you are craftier than any hill-side jackal. Now, if you can do my will, you will have more wealth than ever you won in your life before."

"The offer sounds good in a poor man's ears, King, but it depends upon what is your will."

Ithobal went to the door of the tent, and commanded the sentries who stood without to suffer none to disturb him or draw near. Then he returned and said:—

"I will tell you, but beware that you do not betray my counsels in this or in any other matter, for I have sharp ears and a long arm. You know how things are between me and the lady Elissa and her father Sakon and the city which he governs. They stand thus: Unless within eight days she is given to me in marriage, I have sworn that I will make war upon Zimboe. Ay, and I will make it, for, filled with hate for the white man, already the great tribes are gathering to my banners in ten armies, each of them ten thousand strong. Once let them march beneath yonder walls, and before they leave it Zimboe, city of gold, shall be nothing but a heap of ruins, and a habitation of the dead. Such shall be my vengeance; but I seek love more than vengeance, for what will it avail me to butcher all that people of traders if—as well may chance in the accidents of war—I lose her whom I desire, whose beauty shall be my crown of crowns, and whose mind shall make me great indeed?

"Therefore, Metem, if may be, I would win her without war; let the war come afterwards, as come it must, for the time is ripe. And though she turned from me, this I should have done, had it not been for yonder prince Aziel, whom she met in a strange fashion, and straightway learned to love. Now the thing is more difficult. Nay, while the prince Aziel can take her to wife it is well-nigh impossible, since no threats of war or ruin can turn a woman's heart from him she seeks—to him she flies. Therefore, I ask you—"

"Your pardon, King," Metem broke in, "I see that you, like your rival, are so besotted with the beauty of this girl, that in all with which she has to do you have lost the rule of your own reason. I would save you perchance from saying words to which I do not wish to listen, and when you find a quiet mind again, that you may regret having spoken. If you were about to require of me that I should cause or be privy to the death of the prince Aziel, you would require it in vain; yes, even if you were willing to pay me gold in mountains, and gems in camel loads. With murder I will have nothing to do; moreover, the prince, your rival, is my friend and master, and I will not harm him. Further, I may tell you that after the adventure of last night none will be able to come near him to hurt a hair of his head, seeing that through daylight and through darkness he is guarded by two men."

"With a woman's body to set before him as a shield," said Ithobal bitterly. "But you speak too fast; I was not about to ask you to kill this man, or even to procure his death, because I know it would be useless, but rather that you should so contrive that he cannot take Elissa. How you contrive it I care nothing, so that she is not harmed. You may kidnap him, or stir up the city against him, as one destined to be the source of war, and cause him to be despatched back to the great sea, or bribe the priests of El to hide him away, or what you will, if only you separate him from this woman for ever. Say, merchant, are you willing to undertake the task, or must my good gold go elsewhere?"

Metem pondered awhile and answered:—

"I think that I will undertake it, King; that is, if we come to terms, though whether I shall succeed is another matter. I will undertake it not only because I seek to enrich myself, but because I and others who serve him think it is a very evil thing that this prince, Aziel, whose blood is the most royal in the whole world, without the consent of the great king of Israel, his grandfather, should wed the daughter of a Phoenician officer, however beautiful and loving she may be. Also I love yonder city, which I have known for forty years, and would not see it plunged in a bloody war and perhaps destroyed because a certain man desires to call a certain girl his sweetheart. And now if I succeed in this, what will you give me?"

Ithobal named a great sum.

"King," replied Metem, "you must double it, for that amount you speak of I shall be forced to spend in bribes. More; you must give me the gold now, before I leave your camp, or I will do nothing."

"That you may steal it—and do nothing," laughed Ithobal angrily.

"As you will, King. Such are my terms; if they do not please you, well, let me go. But if you accept them, I will sign a bond under which if within eight days I do not make it impossible for the prince Aziel to marry the lady Elissa, you may reclaim so much of the gold as I do not prove to you to have been spent upon your service, and no bond of Metem the Phoenician was ever yet dishonoured. No, on second thought I will learn wisdom from Issachar the Levite and put my hand to no writing which it would pain me that some should read. King, my sworn word must content you. Another thing, soon war may break out, or I may be forced to fly. Therefore, I demand of you a pass sealed with your seal that will enable me to ride with twenty men and all my goods and treasure, even through the midst of your armies. Moreover you shall swear the great oath to me that notice of this pass will be given to your generals and that it shall be respected to the letter. Do you consent to these terms?"

"I consent," said the king presently.

That evening Metem returned to the city of Zimboe, but those who led his two camels little guessed that now they were laden, not with merchandise, but with treasure.

Chapter IX

Greeting to the Baaltis

When Metem accepted bribes from Issachar and from Ithobal, in consideration of his finding means to make the union of Aziel and Elissa impossible, he had already thought out his scheme. It was one which, while promoting, as he considered, the true welfare of the lovers, if successful would separate them effectually and for ever.

It will be remembered that Elissa had explained to the prince how, on the death of the lady Baaltis, another woman was elected by the colleges of the priests and priestesses to fill her place. This lady could marry, indeed she was expected to do so, but her husband must take the title of Shadid, and for her lifetime act as high-priest of El. Therefore, thought Metem, if it could be brought about that Elissa should be chosen as the new Baaltis, it was obvious that there would be an end of the possibility of her marriage to Aziel. Then, in order to wed her, he must renounce his own religion—a thing which no Jew would do—and pose as the earthly incarnation of one whom he considered a false divinity or a devil.

Indeed, not only marriage, but any further intimacy between the pair would be rendered impracticable, for upon this point the religious law, lax enough in many particulars, was very strict. In fact, so strict was it that for the lady Baaltis of the day to be found alone with any man meant death to her and him. The reason of this severity was that she was supposed to represent the goddess; and her husband, the Shadid, a god, so that any questionable behaviour on her part became an insult to the most powerful divinities of Heaven, which could only be atoned by the death of their unworthy incarnations. That these laws were actual and not formal only was proved by the instance that within the hundred years before the birth of Elissa, a lady Baaltis had been executed for some such offence, having been hurled indeed from the topmost pinnacle of the fortress above the temple to the foot of the precipice beneath.

All these sacerdotal customs were familiar to Metem, who argued from them that to procure the nomination of Elissa as the Baaltis would be to build an impassable wall between her and the prince Aziel. Also, by way of compensation, that office would confer upon her the highest dignity and honour which could be attained by any woman in the city. Moreover, her election would place her beyond the reach of the persecutions of Ithobal, since as lady Baaltis she was entitled to choose her own husband without hindrance or appeal, provided only that he was of pure white blood, which Ithobal was not.

Having thought the matter out, and convinced himself that such a course would not only benefit his own pocket, but prove to the lasting advantage of all concerned, Metem, filled with a glow of righteous zeal, set about his task with the promptitude and cunning of his race. It was not an easy task, for although she had enemies and rivals, the daughter of the dead Baaltis, Mesa by name, was considered to be certain of election at the poll of the priests and priestesses. This ceremony was to take place within two days. Nothing discouraged, however, by the scant time at his disposal or other difficulties, without her knowledge or that of her father, Metem began his canvass on behalf of Elissa.

First with a great sum of gold he bought over the ex-Shadid, the husband of the late lady Baaltis. As it chanced, this worthy had quarrelled with his daughter. Therefore it followed that he would prefer to see some stranger chosen in her place in the hope that, notwithstanding his years, by choosing him in marriage she might confirm him in his position of spouse to the goddess.

All Metem's further negotiations need not be followed: money played a part in most of them; jealousy and dislike in some. A few there were also whom he won over by urging the beauty and wisdom of Elissa, and her extraordinary fitness for the post, as evinced by her recent inspiration in the temple! He found his most powerful allies, however, among the members of the council of the city. To these grandees he pointed out that Elissa was a woman of great strength of character, who would certainly never consent to be forced into a marriage with Ithobal, although her refusal should mean a desperate war, and that her father was so much under her influence that he could not be brought to put pressure upon her. Therefore it was obvious that the only way out of the difficulty was her election as Baaltis. This must prove a perfect answer to the suit of the savage king, since the goddess could not be compelled, and even Ithobal, fearing the vengeance of Heaven, would shrink from offering her violence.

There support gained, having first sworn him to secrecy, he attacked Sakon himself, using similar arguments with him. He pointed out, in addition, that if the governor hoped to see his daughter married to prince Aziel, who was in love with her, however dazzling might be the prospects of such a match, it would certainly bring upon him the present wrath of Ithobal, and, in all probability, future trouble with the Courts of Egypt, of Israel, and through them, of Tyre. Thus working in many ways, Metem laboured incessantly to win his end, so that when at last the hour of election came he awaited its issue, fairly confident of success.

It was on this same afternoon that for the first time since she had received the arrow which was meant for his heart, Aziel was admitted to see Elissa. Now at length her recovery was certain, although she had not shaken off her weakness, and her right arm and wrist were still stiff and swollen. Except for two or three of her women, who were seated at their work behind a screen near the far end of the great chamber, she was alone, lying upon a couch in the recess of the window-place. Advancing to her, Aziel bent down to kiss her wounded hand.

"Nay," said Elissa, hiding it beneath the folds of her robe, "it is still black and unsightly with the poison."

"The more reason that I should kiss it, seeing how the stain came there," he answered.

Her eyes met his, and she whispered, "Not my hand, but my brow, Prince, for so I shall be crowned."

He pressed his lips upon her forehead, and replied:—

"Queen of my heart you are already, and though the throne be humble it is sure. The life you saved is yours, and no other's."

"I did but repay a debt," she answered; "but speak of it no more. Gladly would I have died to save you; should such choice arise, would you do so for me, I wonder?"

"There is little need to ask such a question, lady; for your sake I would not only die, I would even endure shame—that is worse than death."

"Sweet words, Aziel," she answered, smiling, "of which we shall learn the value when the hour of trial comes, as come, I think, it will. You told me but now that you were mine, and no other's; but is it so? I have heard the story of a certain princess of Khem with whom your name was mingled. Tell me, if you will, what was it that set you journeying to this far city of ours?"

"The desire to find you," he answered smiling; then seeing that she still looked at him with questioning eyes, he added, "Nay, this is the truth, if you seek truth. Indeed, it is the best that I should tell you, since it seems that already you have heard something of the tale. A while ago I was sent to the Court of the Pharaoh of Egypt, by the will of my grandsire, the king of Israel, upon an embassy of friendship, and to escort thence a certain beautiful princess, my cousin, who was affianced by treaty to an uncle of mine, a great prince of Israel. This I did, showing to the lady courtesy, and no more. But the end of the matter was that when we came to Jerusalem the princess refused to be married to my uncle, to whom she was betrothed—" and he hesitated.

"Nay, be not timid, Prince," said Elissa sharply; "continue, I pray you. I have heard that the lady added somewhat to her refusal."

"That is so, Elissa. She declared before the king that she would wed no man except myself only, whereon my uncle was very angry, and accused me of playing him false, which, indeed, I had not done."

"Although the lady was so fair, Aziel? But what said the great king?"

"He said that never having seen him to whom she was affianced, he would not suffer that she should be forced into marriage with him against her will. Yet that her will might be uninfluenced, he commanded that I should be sent upon a long journey. That was his judgment, lady."

"Yes, but not all of it; surely he added other words?" she broke in eagerly.

"He added," continued Aziel, with some reluctance, "that if while I was on this journey the princess changed her mind, and chose to wed my uncle, it would be well. But, when I returned from it, if she had not changed her mind, and chose—to marry me—then it would be well also, and, though he was little pleased, with this saying my uncle must be satisfied."

"It does not satisfy me, prince Aziel," Elissa answered, the tears starting to her dark eyes. "I know full well that the lady will not change her mind, and take a man who is in years, and whom she hates, in place of one who is young, and whom she loves. Therefore, when you return hence to Jerusalem, by the king's command you will wed her."

"Nay, Elissa; if I am already married that cannot be," he said.

"In Judea, Prince, I am told that men take more wives than one; also, they divorce them," she replied; then added, "Oh, return not there where I shall lose you. If, indeed, you love me, I pray you return not there."

Before he could answer, a sound of singing and of all sorts of music caught Aziel's ear. Looking through the casement, he saw a great procession of the priests and priestesses of El and Baaltis clad in their festal robes and accompanied by many dignitaries of the city, a multitude of people and bands of musicians, advancing across the square towards the door of the palace.

"Why, what passes?" he exclaimed. As he spoke the door opened and two richly arrayed heralds, wands of office in their hands, entered and prostrated themselves before Elissa.

"Greeting to you, most noble and blessed lady, the chosen of the gods!" they cried with one voice. "Prepare, we beseech you, to hear glad tidings, and to receive those who are sent to tell them."

"Glad tidings?" said Elissa. "Has Ithobal then withdrawn his suit?"

"Nay, lady; it is not of Ithobal that the messengers come to speak."

"Then I cannot receive them," she said, sinking back in apprehension. "I am still ill and weak, and I pray to be excused."

"Nay, lady," answered the herald, "that which they have to tell will cure your sickness."

Again Elissa protested. Before the words had left her lips there appeared in the doorway he who had been husband of the dead Baaltis, followed by priests and priestesses, by Sakon her father, with whom was Metem, and many other nobles and dignitaries.

"All hail, lady!" they cried, prostrating themselves before her. "All hail, lady, chosen of the gods!"

Elissa looked at them bewildered.

"Your pardon," she said, "I do not understand."

Then, rising from his knees, he who was still the Shadid until his successor was appointed, addressed her as spokesman.

"Listen," he said, "and learn, lady, the great thing that has befallen you. Know, O divine One, that by the inspiration of El and Baaltis, rulers of the heavens, the colleges of the priests and priestesses of the city, following the voice of the oracles and the pointing of the omens, have set you in that high place which death has emptied. Greeting to you, holder of the spirit of the goddess! Greeting to the Baaltis!"

"I did not seek this honour," she murmured in the silence that followed, "and I refuse it. The throne of the goddess is Mesa's right; let her take it, or if she will not, then find some other woman who is more worthy."

"Lady," said the Shadid, "these words become you well, but it has pleased the gods to choose you and not my daughter, the lady Mesa, or any other woman, and the choice of the gods may not be set aside. Till death shall take you, you and you alone are the lady Baaltis whom we obey."

"Must I then be made divine against my will," she pleaded, and turned to Aziel as though for counsel.

"Be pleased to stand back, prince Aziel," said the stern voice of the Shadid, interposing. "Remember that henceforth no man may speak to the Baaltis save he whom she names with the name of Shadid to be her husband. Henceforward you are parted, since to seek her company would be to cause her death."

Now understanding that the doom of life-long separation had fallen upon them like the sudden sword of fate, Aziel and Elissa gazed at each other in despair. Then, before either of them could speak a word, at a sign from the Shadid, the priestesses closed round Elissa. Throwing a white veil over her head, they broke into a joyful pæan of song, and half-led, half-carried her from the chamber to enthrone her in the palace of the goddess, which was henceforth to be her home.

Presently all the company, including the waiting women, having joined the procession, the chamber was empty, with the exception of Aziel, Metem and Issachar the Levite, who, drawn by the sound of singing, had entered the place unnoticed.

"Take comfort, Prince," said the Phoenician in a half-bantering voice, "if you and the lady Baaltis are truly dear to each other she may still be yours, for you have but to bow the knee to El, and she will name you Shadid and husband."

"Blaspheme not," cried Issachar sternly. "Shall a worshipper of the God of Israel do sacrifice to a demon to win a woman's smile?"

"That time will prove," answered Metem, shrugging his shoulders; "at least it is certain that he will win it in no other way. Prince," he added, changing his tone, "if you have any such thoughts, abandon them, I pray of you, for on this matter the law may not be broken. The man spoke truth, moreover, when he told you that should you be found with the Baaltis, not being her husband, you would cause her death."

Aziel took no notice of his words, but turning to the Levite, he asked in a quiet voice:—

"Did you plot this to separate us, Issachar? If so, you shall live to mourn the deed."

"Listen, Prince," broke in Metem, "it was not Issachar who plotted that the lady Elissa should be chosen Baaltis, but I, or at least I helped the plot. Shall I tell you why I did this? It was to save you and her, and if possible to prevent a great war also. You could not wed this woman who is not of your race, or rank, or religion; and if you could, it would bring about a struggle that must cost thousands their lives, and this city its wealth. Nor could you make of her less than a wife, seeing that she is well-born and that you are her father's guest. Therefore for your own sake it is best that she should be placed beyond your reach. For her sake also it is best, since she is ambitious and born to rule, who henceforth will be clothed with power for all her days. Moreover, had it been otherwise, in the end she must have passed to that savage Ithobal, whom she hates. Now this is scarcely possible, for the lady Baaltis can wed no man who is not of pure white blood, and whom she does not choose of her own free will. That is a decree which may not be broken even by Ithobal. So revile me not, but thank me, though for a little while your heart be sore."

"My heart is sore indeed," answered Aziel, "and if you think your words be wise, their medicine does not soothe, Phoenician. You may have laboured for my welfare and for that of the lady Elissa, or, like the huckster that you are, for your own advantage, or for both—I know not, and do not care to know. But this I know, that you, and Issachar also, are striving to snare Fate in a web of sand, and that Fate will be too strong for it and you. I love this woman and she loves me, because such is our destiny, and no barriers which man may build can serve to separate us. Also of this I am assured, that by your plots you draw the evils you would ward away upon the heads of us all, for from them shall spring war, and deaths, and misery.

"For the rest, do not think, Metem and Issachar, that I, whom you betrayed, and the woman you have ruined with a crown of greatness she did not seek, are clay to be moulded at your will. It is another hand than yours which fashioned the vessel of our destiny; nor can you stay our lips from drinking of the pure wine that fills it. Farewell," and with a grave inclination of the head he left the room.

Metem watched him go, then he turned to Issachar and said:—

"I have earned my hire well, and you must pay the price, but now it troubles me to think that I touched this business. Why it is I cannot say, but it comes upon me that the prince speaks truth, and that no plot of ours can avail to separate these two who were born to each other, although it well may happen that we shall unite them in death alone. Issachar," he added with fierce conviction, "I will not take your gold, for it is the price of blood! I tell you it is the price of blood!"

"Take it or no, as you will, Phoenician," answered the Levite; "at least I am well pleased that the promise of it bought your service. Even should the prince Aziel discharge this day's work with his young life, it is better that he should perish in the body than that he should lose his soul for the bribe of a woman's passing beauty. Whatever else be lost, that is saved to him, since those sorceress lips of hers are set beyond his reach. An Israelite cannot mate with the oracle of Baaltis, Metem."

"You say so, Issachar, but I have seen men climb high to pluck such fruit. Yes, I have seen them climb even when they knew that they must fall before the fruit was reached."

Then he went also, leaving Issachar alone and oppressed with a dread of the future which was none the less real because it could not be defined.

Chapter X

The Embassy

Weak as she was still with recent illness, half-fainting also from the shock of the terrible and unexpected fate which had overtaken her, Elissa was borne in triumph to the palace that now was hers. Around her gilded litter priestesses danced and sang their wild chants, half- bacchanalian and half-religious; before it marched the priests of El, clashing cymbals and crying, "Make way, make way for the new-born goddess! Make way for her whose throne is upon the horned moon!" while all about the multitude of spectators prostrated themselves in worship.

Elissa was borne in triumph. Vaguely she heard the shouts and music, dimly she saw the dancing-girls and the bowing crowds. But all the while her heart was alive with pain and her brain, crushed beneath the menace of this misery, could grasp nothing clearly save the completeness of her loss. Loss! Yes, she was lost indeed. One short hour ago and she was rejoicing in the presence of the man she loved, and who, as she believed, loved her, while in her mind rose visions of some happy life with him far away from this city and the dark rites of the worshippers of Baal. And now she found herself the chief priestess of that worship which already she had learned to fear if not to hate. More, as its priestess, till death should come to comfort her, she was cut off for ever from him whom she adored, cut off also from the hope of that new spiritual light which had begun to dawn upon her soul.

Elissa looked upon the beautiful women who leapt and sang about her litter, listening to the clash of their ornaments of gold, and as she listened and looked her eyes seemed to gain power to behold the spirits within them. Surely she could see these, dark and hideous things, with shifting countenances, terrible to look on, and themselves wearing in their eyes of flame a stamp of eternal terror, while in her ears the music of their golden necklaces was changed to a clank as of fetters and of instruments of torment. Yes; and there before the dancers in the red cloud of dust which rose from their beating feet, floated the dim shape of that demon of whom she had been chosen the high-priestess.

Look at her mocking, inhuman countenance, and her bent brow of power! Look at her spread and flaming hair and her hundred hands outstretched to grasp the souls of men! Hark! the clamour of the cymbals and the cry of the dancers blended together and became her voice, a dreadful voice that gave greeting to her princess, promising her pride of place and life-long power in payment for her service.

"I desire none of these," her heart seemed to answer; "I desire him only whom I have lost."

"Is it so?" replied the Voice. "Then bid him burn incense upon my altar and take him to yourself. Have I not given you enough of beauty to snare a single soul from among the servants of my enemy the God of the Jews?"

"Nay, nay!" her heart cried; "I will not tempt him to do this evil thing."

"Yea, yea!" mocked the phantom Voice; "for your sake he shall burn incense upon my altar."

The phantasy passed, and now the golden gates of the palace of Baaltis rolled open before Elissa. Now, too, the priestesses bore her to the golden throne shaped like a crescent moon, and threw over her a black veil spangled with stars, symbol of the night. Then having shut out the uninitiated, they worshipped her after their secret fashion till she sank down upon the throne overcome with fear and weariness. Then at last they carried her to that wonder of workmanship and allegorical art, the ivory bed of Baaltis, and laid her down to sleep.

At dawn upon the following day an embassy, headed by Sakon, governor of the city, in whose train were Metem and Aziel, went to the camp of Ithobal. The mission of these envoys was to give the king answer to his suit, for he refused to come to Zimboe unless he were allowed to bring a larger force than it was thought prudent to admit into the city gates. At some distance from the tents they halted, while messengers were sent forward inviting Ithobal to a conference on the plain, as it seemed scarcely safe to trust themselves within the stout thorn fence which had been built about the camp. Metem, who said that he had no fear of the king, went with these men, and on reaching the zeriba was at once bidden to the pavilion of Ithobal. He found the great man pacing its length sullenly.

"What seek you here, Phoenician?" he asked, glancing at him over his shoulder.

"My fee, King. The king was pleased to promise me a hundred ounces of gold if I saved the life of the Lady Elissa. I come, therefore, to assure him that my skill has prevailed against the poisoned arrow of that treacherous dog of the desert, which pierced her hand as she spoke with the prince Aziel the other night, and to claim my reward. Here is a note of the amount," and he produced his tablets.

"If half of what I hear is true, rogue," answered Ithobal savagely, "the tormentor and the headsman alone could satisfy all my debt to you. Say, merchant, what return have you made me for that sackful of gold which you bore hence some few days gone?"

"The best of all returns, King," answered Metem cheerfully, although in truth he began to feel afraid. "I have kept my word, and fulfilled the command of the king. I have made it impossible that the prince Aziel should wed the daughter of Sakon."

"Yes, rogue, you have made it impossible by causing her to be consecrated Baaltis, and thus building a barrier which even I shall find too hard to climb. It is scarcely to be hoped that now she will choose me of her own will, and to offer violence to the Baaltis is a sacrilege from which any man—yes, even a king—may shrink, for such deeds draw the curse of Heaven. Know that for this service I am minded to settle my account with you in a fashion of which you have not thought. Have you heard, Phoenician, that the chiefs of certain of my tribes love to decorate their spear-shafts with the hide of white men, and to bray their flesh into a medicine which gives courage to its eater?"

With this pleasing and suggestive query Ithobal paused, and looked towards the door of the tent as though he were about to call his guard.

Now Metem's blood ran cold, for he knew that this royal savage was not one who uttered idle threats. Yet the coolness and cunning which had so often served him well did not fail him in his need.

"I have heard that your people have strange customs," he answered with a laugh, "but I think that even a spear-shaft would scarcely gain beauty from my wrinkled hide, and if anything, the eating of my flesh would make tradesmen and not warriors of your chiefs. Well, let the jest pass, and listen. King, in all my schemings one thought never crossed my mind, namely, that you were a man to suffer scruples to stand between you and the woman you would win. You think that now she is a goddess? Well, if that be so—and it is not for me to say—who could be a fitter mate for the greatest king upon the earth than a goddess from the heavens? Take her, king Ithobal, take her, and this I promise you, that when your armies are encamped without the walls, the priests of El will absolve you of the crime of aspiring to the fair lips of Baaltis."

"The lips of Baaltis," broke in Ithobal; "do you think that I shall find them sweet when another man has rifled them? Secret chambers are many yonder in the palace of the gods, and doubtless the Jew will find his way there."

"Nay, King, for between these two I have indeed built a wall which cannot be climbed. The worshipper of the Lord of Israel may not traffic with the high-priestess of Ashtoreth. Moreover, I shall bring it about that ere long Prince Aziel's face is set seawards."

"Do that, and I will believe you, merchant, though it would be better if you could bring it about that his face was set earthwards, as I will if I can. Well, this time I spare you, though be sure that if aught miscarry, you shall pay the price, how, I have told you. Now I go to talk with these traders, these outlanders, of Zimboe. Why do you wait? You are dismissed and—alive."

Metem looked steadily at the tablets which he still held in his hand.

"I have heard," he said humbly, "that the king Ithobal, the great king, always pays his debts, and as I—an outlander—shall be leaving Zimboe shortly under his safe conduct, I desire to close this small account."

Ithobal went to the door of his tent and commanded that his treasurer should attend him, bringing money. Presently he came, and at his lord's bidding weighed out one hundred ounces of gold.

"You are right, Phoenician," said Ithobal; "I always pay my debts, sometimes in gold and sometimes in iron. Be careful that I owe you no more, lest you who to-day are paid in gold, to-morrow may receive the iron, weighed out in the fashion of which I have spoken. Now, begone."

Metem gathered up the treasure, and hiding it in his ample robe, bowed himself from the royal presence and out of the thorn-hedged camp.

"Without doubt I have been in danger," he said to himself, wiping his brow, "since at one time that black brute, disregarding the sanctity of an envoy, had it in his mind to torture and to kill me. So, so, king Ithobal, Metem the Phoenician is also an honest merchant who 'always pays his debts,' as you may learn in the market-places of Jerusalem, of Sidon and of Zimboe, and I owe you a heavy bill for the fright you have given me to-day. Little of Elissa's company shall you have if I can help it; she is too good for a cross-bred savage, and if before I go from these barbarian lands I can set a drop of medicine in your wine, or an arrow in your gizzard, upon the word of Metem the Phoenician, it shall be done, king Ithobal."

When Metem reached Sakon and the envoys, he found that a message had already been sent to them announcing that Ithobal would meet them presently upon the plain outside his camp. But still the king did not come; indeed, it was not until Sakon had despatched another messenger, saying that he was about to return to the city, that at length Ithobal appeared at the head of a bodyguard of black troops. Arranging these in line in front of the camp, he came forward, attended by twelve or fourteen counsellors and generals, all of them unarmed. Half-way between his own line and that of the Phoenicians, but out of bowshot of either, he halted.

Thereon Sakon, accompanied by a similar number of priests and nobles, among whom were Aziel and Metem, all of them also unarmed, except for the knives in their girdles, marched out to meet him. Their escort they left drawn up upon the hillside.

"Let us to business, King," said Sakon, when the formal words of salutation had passed. "We have waited long upon your pleasure, and already troops move out from the city to learn what has befallen us."

"Do they then fear that I should ambush ambassadors?" asked Ithobal hotly. "For the rest, is it not right that servants should bide at the door of their king till it is his pleasure to open?"

"I know not what they fear," answered Sakon, "but at least we fear nothing, for we are too many," and he glanced at his soldiers, a thousand strong, upon the hillside. "Nor are the citizens of Zimboe the servants of any man unless he be the king of Tyre."

"That we shall put to proof, Sakon," said Ithobal; "but say, what does the Jew with you?" and he pointed to Aziel. "Is he also an envoy from Zimboe?"

"Nay, King," answered the prince laughing, "but my grandsire, the mighty ruler of Israel, charged me always to take note of the ways of savages in peace and war, that I might learn how to deal with them. Therefore, I sought leave to accompany Sakon upon this embassy."

"Peace, peace!" broke in Sakon. "This is no time for gibes. King Ithobal, since you did not dare to venture yourself again within the walls of our city, we have come to answer the demands you made upon us in the Hall of Audience. You demanded that our fortifications should be thrown down, and this we refuse, since we do not court destruction. You demanded that we should cease to enslave men to labour in the mines, and to this we answer that for every man we take we will pay a tax to his lawful chief, or to you as king. You demanded that the ancient tribute should be doubled. To this, out of love and friendship, and not from fear, we assent, if you will enter into a bond of lasting peace, since it is peace we seek, and not war. King, you have our answer."

"Not all of it, Sakon. How of that first condition—that Lady Elissa the fair, your daughter, should be given me to wife?"

"King, it cannot be, for the gods of heaven have taken this matter from our hands, anointing the lady Elissa their high-priestess."

"Then as I live," answered Ithobal with fury, "I will take her from the hands of the gods and anoint her my dancing-woman. Do you think to make a mock of me, you people of Zimboe, whom I have honoured by desiring one of your daughters in marriage? You seek to trick me with your priests' juggling that you may keep her to be the toy of yonder princeling? So be it, but I tell you that I will tear your city stone from stone, and anoint its ruins with your blood. Yes, your young men shall labour in the mines for me, and your high-born maidens shall wait upon my queens. Listen, you"—and he turned to his generals—"Let the messengers who are ready start east and west, and north and south, to the chiefs whose names you have, bidding them to meet me with their tribesmen, at the time and place appointed. When next I speak with you, Elders of Zimboe, it shall be at the head of a hundred thousand warriors."

"Then, King, on your hands be all the innocent lives that these words of yours have doomed, and may the weight of their wasted blood press you down to ruin and death."

Thus answered Sakon proudly, but with pale lips, for do what they would to hide it, something of the fear they felt for the issue of this war was written on the faces of all his company.

Ithobal turned upon his heel, deigning no reply, but as he went he whispered a word into the ear of two of his captains, great men of war, who stayed behind the rest of his party searching for something upon the ground. Sakon and his counsellors also turned, walking towards their escort, but Aziel lingered a little, fearing no danger, and being curious to learn what the men sought.

"What do you seek, captains?" he asked courteously.

"A gold armlet that one of us has lost," they answered.

Aziel let his eyes wander on the ground, and not far away perceived the armlet half-hidden in a tussock of dry grass, where, indeed, it had been placed.

"Is this the ring?" he asked, lifting it and holding it towards them.

"It is, and we thank you," they answered, advancing to take the ornament.

The next moment, before Aziel even guessed their purpose, the captains had gripped him by either arm and were dragging him at full speed towards their camp. Understanding their treachery and the greatness of his danger, he cried aloud for help. Then throwing himself swiftly to the ground, he set his feet against a stone that chanced to lie in their path in such fashion that the sudden weight tore his right arm from the group of the man that held him. Now, quick as thought, Aziel drew the dagger from his girdle, and, still lying upon his back, plunged it into the shoulder of the second man so that he loosed him in his pain. Next he sprang to his feet, and, leaping to one side to escape the rush of his captors, ran like a deer towards the party of Sakon, who had wheeled round at the sound of his cry.

Ithobal and his men had turned also and sped towards them, but at a little distance they halted, the king shouting aloud:—

"I desired to hold this foreigner, who is the cause of war between us, hostage for your daughter's sake, Sakon, but this time he has escaped me. Well, it matters nothing, for soon my turn will come. Therefore, if you and he are wise, you will send him back to the sea, for thither alone I promise him safe conduct."

Then without more words he walked to his camp, the gates of which were closed behind him.

"Prince Aziel," said Sakon, as they went towards the city, "it is ill to speak such words to an honoured guest, but it cannot be denied that you bring much trouble on my head. Twice now you have nearly perished at the hands of Ithobal, and should that chance, doubtless I must earn the wrath of Israel. On your behalf, also, the city of Zimboe is this day plunged into a war that well may be her last, since it is because you have grown suddenly dear to her that my daughter has continued to refuse the suit of Ithobal, and because of his outraged pride at this refusal that he has raised up the nations against us. Prince, while you remain in this city there is no hope of peace. Do not, therefore, hate me, your servant, if I pray of you to leave us while there is yet time."

"Sakon," answered Aziel, "I thank you for your open speech, and will pay you back in words as honest as your own. Gladly would I go, for here nothing but sorrow has befallen me, were it not for one thing which to you may seem little, but to me, and perhaps to another, is all in all. I love your daughter as I have never loved a woman before, and as my mind is to hers, so is hers to mine. How, then, can I go hence when the going means that I must part from her for ever?"

"How can you stay here, Prince, when the staying means that you must bring her to shame and death, and yourself with her? Say now, are you prepared, for the sake of this maiden, to abandon the worship of your fathers and to become the servant of El and Baaltis?"

"You know well that I am not so prepared, Sakon. For nothing that the world could give me would I do this sin."

"Then, Prince, it is best that you should go, for that and no other is the price you must pay if you would win my daughter Elissa. Should you seek to do so by other means, I tell you that neither your high rank nor the power of my rule and friendship, nor pity for your youth and hers, can save you both from death, since to forgive you then would be to bring down the wrath of its outraged gods upon Zimboe. Oh! Prince, for your own sake and for the sake of her whom both you and I love thus dearly, linger no longer in temptation, but turn your back upon it as a brave man should, for so shall my blessing follow you to the grave and your years be filled with honour."

Aziel covered his eyes with his hand, and thought a while; then he answered:—

"Be it as you will, friend. I go, but I go broken-hearted."

Chapter XI

Metem Sells Images

Upon reaching the palace, Aziel went to the apartments of Issachar. Finding no keeper at the door, he entered, to discover the old priest kneeling in prayer at the window, which faced towards Jerusalem. So absorbed was he in his devotions that it was not until he had ended them and risen that Issachar saw Aziel standing in the chamber.

"Behold, an answer to my prayer," he said. "My son, they told me that some fresh danger had overtaken you, though none knew its issue. Therefore it was that I prayed, and now I see you unharmed." And taking him in his arms, he embraced him.

"It is true that I have been in danger, father," answered Aziel, and he told him the story of his escape from Ithobal.

"Did I not pray thee not to accompany this embassy?"

"Yes, father, yet I have returned in safety. Listen: I come with tidings which you will think good. Not an hour ago I promised Sakon that I would leave Zimboe, where it seems my presence breeds much trouble."

"Good tidings, indeed!" exclaimed Issachar, "and never shall I know a peaceful hour until we have seen the last of the towers of this doomed city and its accursed people of devil-worshippers."

"Yes, good for you, father, but for me most ill, for here I shall leave my youth and happiness. Nay, I know what you think; that this is but some passing fancy bred of the pleasant beauty of a woman, but it is not so. I say that from the moment when first I saw Elissa, she became life of my life, and soul of my soul and that I go hence beggared of joy and hope, and carrying with me a cankering memory which shall eat my heart away. You deem her a witch, one to whom Baaltis has given power to drag the minds of men to their destruction, but I tell you that her only spell is the spell of her love for me, also that she whom you named so grossly is no longer the servant of the demon Baaltis."

"Elissa not the servant of Baaltis? How comes she then to be her high-priestess? Aziel, your passion has made you mad."

'She is high-priestess because Metem and others brought about her election without her will, urged on to it by I know not whom." And he looked hard at Issachar, who turned away. "But what matters it who did the ill deed," he continued, "since this, at least, is certain, that here my presence breeds sorrow and bloodshed, and therefore I must go as I have promised."

"When do we depart, Prince?" queried Issachar.

"I know not, it is naught to me. Here comes Metem, ask of him."

"Metem," said the Levite, "the prince desires to leave Zimboe and march to the coast, there to take ship to Tyre. When can your caravan be ready?"

"So I have heard, Issachar, for Sakon tells me that he has come to an agreement with the prince upon this matter. Well, I am glad to learn it, for troubles thicken here, and I think that the woe you prophesied is not far from this city of Zimboe where every man seeks to serve his own hand, and is ready to sell his neighbour. When can the caravan be got ready? Well, the night after next; at least, we can start that night. To-morrow evening, so soon as the sun is down, I will send on the camels by ones and twos, and with them the baggage and treasure, to a secret place I know of in the mountains, where we and the prince's guard can follow upon the mules and join them. As it chances, I have a safe conduct from Ithobal. Still I should not wish to put his troops into temptation by marching through them with twenty laden camels, or to lose certain earnings of my own that will be hidden in the baggage. Moreover, if our departure becomes known, half the city would wish to join us, having no love of soldiering, and misdoubting them much of the issue of this war with Ithobal."

"As you will," said Issachar, "you are captain of the caravan, and charged with the safety of the prince upon his journeyings. I am ready whenever you appoint, and the quicker that hour comes, the more praise you will have from me."

"Come with me, I wish to speak with you," said Aziel to the Phoenician as they left the presence of Issachar. "Listen," he added, when they had reached his chamber, "we leave this city soon, and I have farewells to make."

"To the Baaltis?" suggested Metem.

"To the lady Elissa. I desire to send her a letter of farewell; can you deliver it into her own hand?"

"It may be managed, Prince, at a price—nay, from you I ask no price. I have still some images that I wish to sell, and we merchants go everywhere, even into the presence of the Baaltis if it pleases her to admit them. Write your scroll and I will take it, though, to be plain, it is not a task which I should have sought."

So Aziel wrote slowly and with care. Then having sealed the writing he gave it to Metem.

"Your face is sat, Prince," he said, as he hid it in his robe, "but, believe me, you are doing what is right and wise."

"It may be so," answered Aziel, "yet I would rather die than do it, and may my curse lie heavy upon the heads of those who have so wrought that it must be done. Now, I pray you, deliver this scroll into the hands of her you know, and bring me the answer if there be any, betraying it to none, for I will double whatever sum is offered for that treachery."

"Have no fear, Prince," said Metem quietly, but without taking offence, "this errand is undertaken for friendship, not for profit. The risk is mine alone; the gain—or loss—is yours."

An hour later the Phoenician stood in the palace of the gods, demanding, under permit from Sakon, governor of the city, to be admitted into the presence of the Baaltis, to whom he desired to sell certain sacred images cunningly fashioned in gold. Presently it was announced that he was allowed to approach, and the officers of the temple led him through guarded passages, to the private chambers of the priestesses. Here he found Elissa in a long, low hall, sweet with scented woods, rich with gold, and supported by pillars of cedar.

She was seated alone at the far end of this hall, beneath the window- plate, clad in her white robes of office, richly broidered with emblems of the moon. Her women, most of whom were employed in needle- work, though some whispered idly to each other, were gathered at the lower end of the hall near to its door.

Metem saluted them as he entered, and they detained him, answering his greeting by requests for news and with jests, not too refined, or by demands for presents of jewels, in return for which they promised him the blessings of the goddess. To each he made some apt reply, for even the priestesses of Baaltis could not abash Metem. But while he bandied words, his quick eyes noted one of their number who did not join in this play. She was a spare, thin-lipped woman whom he knew for Mesa, the daughter of the dead Baaltis, who had been a rival candidate for the throne of the high-priestess when Elissa was chosen in her place.

When he entered the hall Mesa was seated upon a canvas stool, a little apart from the others, her chin resting upon her hand, staring with an evil look towards the place where Elissa was enthroned. Nor did her face grow more gentle at the sight of the cunning merchant, for she knew well it was through his plots and bribery that she had been ousted from her mother's place.

"A woman to be feared," thought Metem to himself as, shaking off the priestesses, he passed her upon his way up the long chamber. Presently he had reached the end of it, and was saluting the presence of the Baaltis by kneeling and touching the carpet with his brow.

"Rise, Metem," said Elissa, "and set out your business, for the hour of the sunset prayer is at hand, and I cannot talk long with you."

So he rose, and, looking at her while he laid out his store of images, saw that her face was sad, and that her eyes were full of a strange fear.

"Lady," he said, "on the second night from now I depart from this city of yours, and glad shall I be to leave it living. Therefore I have brought you these four priceless images of the most splendid workmanship of Tyre, thinking that it might please you to purchase them for the service of the goddess."

"You depart," she whispered; "alone?"

"No lady, not alone; the holy Issachar goes with me, also the escort of the prince Aziel—and the prince himself, whose presence is no longer desired in Zimboe." Here he stopped, for he saw that Elissa was about to betray her agitation, and whispered, "Be not foolish, for you are watched; I have a letter for you. Lady," he continued in a louder voice, "if it will please you to examine this precious image in the light, you will no longer hesitate or think the price too high," and bowing low he led the way behind the throne, whither Elissa followed him.

Now they were standing beneath the window-place, which they faced, and hidden from the gaze of the women by the gilded back of the high seat.

"Here," he said, thrusting the parchment into her hand, "read quickly, and return it to me."

She snatched the roll from him, and as her eyes devoured the lines, her face fell in, and her lips grew pale with anguish.

"Be brave," murmured Metem, for his heart was stirred to pity; "it is best for all that he should go."

"For him, perchance it is best," she answered; as with an unwilling hand she gave him back the letter which she dared not keep, "but what of me? Oh! Metem, what of me?"

"Lady," he said sadly, "I have no words to soothe your sorrow save that the gods have willed it thus."

"What gods?" she asked fiercely; "not those they bid me worship." She shuddered, then went on, "Metem, be pitiful! Oh! if ever you have loved a woman, or have been loved of one, for her sake be pitiful. I must see him for the last time in farewell, and you can help me to it."

"I! In the name of Baal, how?"

"When do you have to leave the city, Metem?"

"At moonrise on the night after next."

"Then an hour before moonrise I will be in the temple, whither I can come by the secret way that leads thither from this palace, and he can enter there, for the little gate shall be left unbarred. Pray him to meet me, then—for the last time."

"Lady," he urged, "this is but madness, and I refuse. You must find another messenger."

"Madness or not it is my will, and beware how you thwart me in it, Metem, for at least I am the Lady Baaltis, and have power to kill without question. I swear to you that if I do not see him, you shall never leave this city living."

"A shrewd argument, and to the point," said Metem reflectively. "Well, I have prepared myself a rock-hewn tomb at Tyre, and do not wish that my graven sarcophagus of best Egyptian alabaster should be wasted, or sold to some upstart for a song."

"As assuredly it will be, if you do not obey me in this matter, Metem. Remember—an hour before moonrise, at the foot of the pillar of El in the inner court of the temple."

As she spoke Metem started, for his quick ears had caught a sound.

"O Queen divine," he said in a loud voice, as he led the way to the front of the throne, "you are a hard bargainer! Were there many such, a poor trader could not make a living. Ah! here is one who knows the value of such priceless works of art," and he pointed to Mesa, who, with folded arms and downcast eyes, stood within five paces of the throne, as near, indeed, as custom allowed her to approach. "Lady," he went on addressing you, "you will have heard the price I asked; say, now, is it too much?"

"I have heard nothing, sir. I stand here, waiting the return of my holy mistress that I may remind her that the hour of sunset prayer is at hand."

"Would that I had so fair a mentor," exclaimed Metem, "for then I should lose less time." But to himself he said, "She has heard something, though I think but little," then added aloud: "Well judge between us, lady. Is fifty golden shekels too much for these images which have been blessed and sprinkled with the blood of children by the high priest of Baal at Sidon?"

Mesa lifted her cold eyes and looked at them. "I think it too much," she said, "but it is for the lady Baaltis to judge. Who am I that I should open my lips in the presence of the lady Baaltis?"

"I have appealed to the oracle, and it has spoken against me," said Metem, wringing his hands in affected dismay. "Well, I abide the result. Queen, you offered me forty shekels and for forty you shall take them, for the honour of the holy gods, though in truth I lose ten shekels by the bargain. Give your order to the treasurer, and he will pay me to-morrow. So now farewell," and bowing till his forehead touched the ground, he kissed the hem of her robe.

Elissa bent her head in acknowledgment of the salute, and as he rose her eyes met his. In them was written a warning which he could not fail to understand, and although she did not speak, her lips seemed to shape the word, "Remember."

Ten minutes later Metem stood in the chamber of Aziel.

"Has she seen the letter, and what did she answer?" asked the prince, springing up almost as he passed the threshold.

"In the name of all the gods of all the nations I pray you not to speak so loud," answered Metem when he had closed the door and looked suspiciously about him. "Oh! if ever I find myself safe in Tyre again, I vow a gift, and no mean one, to each of them that has a temple there, and they are many; for no single god is strong enough to bring me safe out of this trouble. Have I seen the lady Elissa? Oh, yes, I have seen her. And what think you that this innocent lamb, this undefiled dove of yours, threatens me with now? Death! nothing less than death, if I will not carry out her foolish wishes. More, she means the threat, and has the strength to fulfil it, for to the lady Baaltis is given power over the lives of men, or at the least, if she takes life none question the authority of the goddess. Unless I do her will I am a dead man, and that is the reward I get for mixing myself up in your mad love affairs."

"Hold!" broke in Aziel, "and tell me, man, what is her will?"

"Her will is—what do you think? To meet you in farewell an hour before you leave this city. Well, as my throat is at stake, by Baal! it shall be gratified if I can find the means, though I tell you that it is madness and nothing else. But listen to the story—" and he repeated all that had passed. "Now," he added, "are you ready to take the risk, Prince?"

"I should be a coward indeed if I did not," answered Aziel, "when she, a woman, dares a heavier."

"And I am a coward, that is why I take it, for otherwise I also must dare a heavier. But what of Issachar? This meeting can scarcely be kept a secret from him."

Aziel thought awhile and said:—

"Go fetch him here." So Metem went, to return presently with the Levite, to whom, without further ado, the prince told all, hiding nothing.

Issachar listened in silence. When both Aziel and Metem had done speaking, he said:—

"At least, I thank you, Prince, for being open with me; and now without more words I pray you to abandon this rash plan, which can end only in pain, and perhaps in death."

"Abandon it not, Prince," interrupted Metem, "seeing that if you do it will certainly end in my death, for the girl is mad, and will have her way. Or if she does not, then I must pay the price."

"Have no fear," answered Aziel smiling. "Issachar, this must be done or—"

"Or what, Prince?"

"I will not leave the city. It is true that Sakon may thrust me from it, but it shall be as a dead man. Nay, waste no words, since she desires it; I must and will meet the Lady Elissa for the last time, not as lover meets lover, but as those meet who part for ever in the world."

"You say so, Prince; then have I your permission to accompany you?"

"Yes, if you wish it, Issachar; but there is danger."

"Danger! What care I for danger? The will of Heaven be done to me. So be it, we will go together, but the end of it is not with us."

Chapter XII

The Tryst

Two days had gone by, and at the appointed hour three figures, wrapped in dark cloaks, might have been seen walking swiftly towards the little entrance of the temple fortress. Although it was near to midnight the city was still astir with men, for this very evening news had reached it that Ithobal was advancing at the head of tens of thousands of the warriors of the Tribes. More, it was rumoured freely that within the next few days the siege of Zimboe would begin. Late as it was, the council had been just summoned to the palace of Sakon to consider the conduct of the defence, while in every street stood knots of men engaged in anxious discussion, and from many a smithy rose the sound of armourers at their work. Here marched parties of soldiers of various races, there came long strings of mules laden with dried flesh and grain; yonder a woman beat her breast, and wept loudly because her three sons had been impressed by order of the council, two of them to serve as archers and the third to carry blocks of stone for the fortifications.

Passing unnoticed through all this crowd and tumult, Aziel, Issachar and Metem entered a winding passage in the temple wall, and came to the little gate. Metem tried it, and whispered:—

"She has kept her word; it is unlocked. Now enter to your love-tryst, holy Issachar."

"Do you not come with us?" asked the Levite.

"No, I am too old for such adventures. Listen, I go to make ready. Within an hour the mules with the prince's bodyguard will stand in the archway near the small gate of the palace, for by now the baggage and its escort await us a day's march from this accursed city. Will you meet me there? No; I think it is best that I should come to your chambers to fetch you, and, I pray you, let there be no delay, for it is dangerous in many ways. When once the prince has done with his tender interview, and wiped away his tears, there should be nothing to stay him, since the farewell cup with Sakon has been already drunk. Enter now swiftly before some prowling priest happens upon you, and pray that you may come out as sound as you go in. Oh! what a sight! A prince of Israel and an aged Levite of established reputation going to keep a tryst at midnight with the high-priestess of Baaltis in the sanctuary of her god! Nay, answer not; there is no time"—and he was gone.

Having passed the gate, Aziel and Issachar crept down the winding passages of stone, groping their path by such light as fell from the narrow line of sky above them, till at length they reached the court of the sanctuary. Here the place was as silent as death, for the noise from the city without could not pierce its towering walls of massive granite.

"It is the very pit of Tophet," murmured Issachar, peering through the dense shadows, "the house of Beelzebub, where his presence dwells. Whither now, Aziel?"

The prince pointed to two objects that were visible in the starlight, and answered:—

"Thither, at the foot of the pillar of El."

"Ah! I remember," said Issachar, "where the accursed woman would have offered sacrifice, and the priests struck me down because I prophesied to them of the wrath to come, and that is now at hand. An ill-omened spot, indeed, and an ill-omened tryst with the fiends for witnesses. Well, lead on, and I pray you to be brief as may be, for this place weighs down my soul, and I feel danger in it—danger to the body and the spirit."

So they went forward. "Be careful," whispered Aziel presently. "The pit of sacrifice is at your feet."

"Yes, yes," he answered, "we walk upon the edge of the pit, and, in truth, I grow fearful, for at the threshold of such places the angel of the Lord deserts us."

"There is nothing to fear," said Aziel. But even as he spoke, although he could not see it, a white face rose above the edge of the pit, like that of some ghost struggling from the tomb, watched them a moment with cold eyes, then disappeared again.

Now they were near the greater pillar, and now from its shadow glided a black-veiled shape.

"Elissa?" murmured Aziel.

"It is I," whispered a soft voice; "but who comes with you?"

"I, Issachar," said the Levite, "who would not suffer that he of whom I am given charge should seek such company alone. Now, priestess, say your say with the prince yonder and let us be gone swiftly from this blood-stained place."

"You speak harsh words to me, Issachar," she said gently, "yet I am most glad that you have come, for, believe me, I sought no lovers' meeting with the prince Aziel. Listen, both of you: you know that they have consecrated me high-priestess of Baaltis against my will. Now, I tell you, Issachar, what I have already told the prince Aziel—that I am no longer a worshipper of Baaltis. Yes, here in her very temple I renounce her, even though she takes my life in vengeance. Oh! since they made me priestess I have been forced to learn all her worship, which before I never even guessed, and to see sights that would chill your blood to hear of them. Now I tell you, prince Aziel and Issachar, that I will bear no more. From El and Baaltis I turn to Him you worship, though, alas! little time is left to me in which to plead for pardon."

"Why is little time left?" broke in Aziel.

"Because my death is very near me, Prince, for if I live, see what a fate is mine. Either I must remain high-priestess of Baaltis and to her day by day bow the knee, and month by month make sacrifice—of what think you? Well, to be plain, of the blood of maids and children. Or, perhaps, should their fears overcome their scruples, I shall be given by the council as a peace-offering to Ithobal.

"I say that I will bear neither of these burdens of blood or shame; they are too heavy for me. Prince, so soon as you are gone I too shall leave this city, not in the body, but in the spirit, searching for peace or sleep. It was for this reason that I sought to speak with you in farewell, since in my weakness I desired that you should learn the truth of the cause and manner of my end.

"Now you know all, and as for me there is no escape, farewell for ever, prince Aziel, whom I have loved, and whom I can scarcely hope to meet again, even beyond the grave." Then with a little despairing motion of her hand she turned to go.

"Stay," said Aziel hoarsely, "we cannot be parted thus; since by your own act you can dare to leave the world, will you not dare to fly this place with me?"

"Perhaps, Prince," she answered with a little laugh, "but would you dare to take me, and if so, would Issachar here suffer it? No, no; go your own path in life, and leave me death—it is the easier way."

"In this matter I am master and not Issachar," said Aziel, "though it be true that should it please him, he can warn the priests of El. Listen, Elissa: either you leave this city with me, or I stay in it with you. You hear me, Issachar?"

"I hear you," said the Levite, "but perchance before you throw more sharp words at my head, you will suffer me to speak. Self-murder is a crime, yet I honour this woman who would shed her own blood, rather than the blood of the innocent in sacrifice to Baal, and who refuses to be given in marriage to one she hates; who, moreover, has found strength and grace to trample on her devil-worship, if so in truth she has. If therefore she will come with us and we can escape with her, why, let her come. Only swear to me, Aziel, that you will make no wife of her till the king, your grandsire, has heard this tale and given judgment on it."

"That I will swear for him," exclaimed Elissa; "is it not so, Aziel?"

"As you will, lady," he answered. "Issachar, you have my word that until then she shall be as my sister, and no more."

"I hear and I believe you," said Issachar, adding: "And now, lady, we go at once, so if you desire to accompany us, come."

"I am ready," she replied, "and the hour is well chosen for I shall not be missed till dawn."

So they turned and left the temple. None stayed or hindered them, yet although they reached the chambers of Aziel in safety, their hearts, which should have been light, were still heavy with the presage of new sorrow to come.

Scarcely could they have been heavier, indeed, had they seen a white- faced woman creep from the pit of death and follow them stealthily till they had passed from the temple into the palace doors, then turn and run at full speed towards the college of the priests of El.

In the chamber of Aziel they found Metem.

"I rejoice to see you back again in safety, since it is more than I thought to do," he said, while they entered, adding, as the black- veiled shape of Elissa followed them into the room, "but who is the third? Ah! I see, the lady Elissa. Does the Baaltis accompany us upon our journey?"

"Yes," answered Aziel shortly.

"Then with her high Grace on the one side and the holy Issachar on the other it should not lack for blessings. Surely that evil must be great from which, separately or together, they are unable to defend us. But, lady, if I may ask it, have you bid farewell to your most honoured father?"

"Torment me not," murmured Elissa.

"Indeed, I did not wish to, though you may remember that not so long ago you threatened to silence me for ever. Well, doubtless your departure is too hurried for farewells, and, fortunately, foreseeing it, I have provided spare mules. So my deeds are kinder than my words. I go to see that all is prepared. Now eat before you start; presently I will return for you," and he left the chamber.

When he had gone they gathered round the table on which stood food, but could touch little of it; for the hearts of all three of them were filled with sad forebodings. Soon they heard a noise as of people talking excitedly outside the palace gates.

"It is Metem with the mules," said Aziel.

"I hope so," answered Elissa.

Again there was silence, which, after a while, was broken by a loud knocking at the door.

"Rise," said Aziel, "Metem comes for us."

"No, no," cried Elissa, "it is Doom that knocks, not Metem."

As the words passed her lips the door was burst open, and through it poured a mob of armed priests, at the head of whom marched the Shadid. By his side was his daughter Mesa, in whose pale face the eyes burned like torches in a wind.

"Did I not tell you so?" she said in a shrill voice, pointing at the three. "Behold the Lady Baaltis and her lover, and with them that priest of a false faith who called down curses upon our city."

"You told us indeed, daughter," answered the Shadid; "pardon us if we were loth to believe that such a thing could be." Then with a cry of rage he added, "Take them."

Now Aziel drew his sword, and sprang in front of Elissa to protect her, but before he could strike a blow it was seized from behind, and he was gripped by many hands, gagged, bound and blindfolded. Then like a man in a dream he felt himself carried away through long passages, till at length he reached an airless place, where the gag and bandages were removed.

"Where am I?" Aziel asked.

"In the vaults of the temple," answered the priests as they left the prison, barring its great door behind them.

Chapter XIII

The Sacrilege of Aziel

How long he lay in his dungeon, lost in bitter thought and tormented by fears for Elissa, Aziel could not tell, for no light came there to mark the passage of the hours. In the tumult of his mind, one terrible thought grew clear and ever clearer; he and Elissa had been taken red- handed, and must pay the price of their sin against the religious customs of the city. For the Baaltis to be found with any man who was not her husband meant death to him and her, a doom from which there was little chance of escape.

Well, to his own fate he was almost indifferent, but for Elissa and Issachar he mourned bitterly. Truly the Levite and Metem had been wise when they cautioned him, for her sake and his own, to have nothing to do with a priestess of Baal. But he had not listened; his heart would not let him listen—and now, unless they were saved by a miracle—or Metem—in the fulness of their youth and love, the lives of both of them were forfeited.

Worn out with sore fears and vain regrets Aziel fell at length into a heavy sleep. He was awakened by the opening of the door of his dungeon, and the entry of priests—grim, silent men who seized and blindfolded him. Then they led him away up many stairs, and along paths so steep that from time to time they paused to rest, till at length he knew, by the sound of voices, that he had reached some place where people were assembled. Here the bandage was removed from his eyes. He stepped backwards, recoiling involuntarily at the glare of light that poured upon him from the setting sun, whereon, uttering an exclamation, those who stood near seized and held him. Presently he saw the reason. He was standing on the brink of a precipice at the back of and dominating the dim and shadow-clad city, while far beneath him lay a gloomy rift along which ran the trade road to the coast.

Here in this dizzy spot was a wide space of rock, walled in upon three sides. The precipice formed the fourth side of its square, in which, seated upon stones that seemed to have been set there in semi-circles to serve as judgment chairs, were gathered the head priests and priestesses of El and Baaltis, clad in their sacerdotal robes. To the right and left of these stood knots of favoured spectators, among whom Aziel recognised Metem and Sakon, while at his side, but separated from him by armed priests, were Elissa herself, wrapped in a dark veil, and Issachar. Lastly, in front of him, a fire flickered upon a little altar, and behind the altar stood a shrine containing a symbolical effigy of Baaltis fashioned of gold, ivory and wood to the shape of a woman with a hundred breasts.

Seeing all this, Aziel understood that they three had been brought here for trial, and that the priests and priestesses before him were their judges. Indeed, he remembered that the place had been pointed out to him as one where those who had offended against the gods were carried for judgment. Thence, if found guilty, such unfortunates were hurled down the face of the precipice and left, a shapeless mass of broken bone, to crumble on the roadway at its foot.

After a long and solemn pause, at a sign from the Shadid, he who had been the husband of the dead Baaltis, the veil was removed from Elissa. At once she turned, looked at Aziel, and smiled sadly.

"Do you know the fate that waits us?" the prince asked of Issachar in Hebrew.

"I know, and I am ready," answered the old Levite, "for since my soul is safe I care little what these dogs may do to my body. But, oh! my son, I weep for you, and cursed be the hour when first you saw that woman's face."

"Spare to reproach me in my misfortune," murmured Elissa; "have I not enough to bear, knowing that I have brought death upon him I love? Oh! curse me not, but pray that my sins may be forgiven me."

"That I will do gladly, daughter," replied Issachar more gently, "the more so that, although you seem to be the cause of them, these things can have happened only by the will of Heaven. Therefore I was wrong to revile you, and I ask your pardon."

Before she could answer the Shadid commanded silence. At the same moment the woman Mesa stepped from behind the effigy of the goddess on the shrine.

"Who are you and what do you here?" asked the Shadid, as though he did not know her.

"I am Mesa, the daughter of her who was the lady Baaltis," she answered, "and my rank is that of Mother of the priestesses of Baaltis. I appear to give true evidence against her, who is the anointed Baaltis, against the Israelitish stranger named Aziel, and the priest of the Lord of the Jews."

"Lay your hand upon the altar and speak, but beware what you speak," said the Shadid.

Mesa bowed her head, took the oath of truth by touching the altar with her fingers, and began:—

"From the time that she was appointed I have been suspicious of the lady Baaltis."

"Why were you suspicious?" asked the Shadid.

The witness let her eyes wander towards Metem, then hesitated. Evidently for some reason of her own she did not wish to implicate him.

"I was suspicious," she answered, "because of certain words that came from the lips of the Baaltis, when she had been thrown into the holy trance before the fire of sacrifice. As is my accustomed part, I bent over her to hear and to announce the message of the gods, but in place of the hallowed words there issued babblings about this Hebrew stranger and of a meeting to be held with him at one hour before moonrise by the pillar of El in the courtyard of the temple. Thereafter for several nights as was my duty I hid myself in the pit of offerings in the courtyard and watched. Last night at an hour before the moonrise the Lady Baaltis came disguised by the secret way and waited at the pillar, where presently she was joined by the Jew Aziel and the Levite, who spoke with her.

"What they said I could not hear, because they were too far from me, but at length they left the temple and I traced them to the chambers of the Jew Aziel, in the palace of Sakon. Then, Shadid, I warned you, and the priests and you accompanied me and took them. Now, as Mother of the priestesses, I demand that justice be done upon these wicked ones, according to the ancient custom, lest the curse of Baaltis should fall upon this city."

When she had finished her evidence, with a cold stare of triumphant hate at her rival, Mesa stepped to one side.

"You have heard," said the Shadid addressing his fellow-judges. Do you need further testimony? If so, it must be brief, for the sun sinks."

"Nay," answered the spokesman, "for with you we took the three of them together in the chamber of the prince Aziel. Set out the law of this matter, O Judge, and let justice be done according to the strict letter of the law—justice without fear or favour."

"Hearken," said the Shadid. "Last night this woman Elissa, the daughter of Sakon, being the lady Baaltis duly elected, met men secretly in the courts of the temple and accompanied them, or one of them, to the chamber of Aziel, a prince of Israel, the guest of Sakon. Whether or no she was about to fly with him from the city which he should have left last night, we cannot tell, and it is needless to inquire, at least she was with him. This, however, is sure, that they did not sin in ignorance of our law, since with my own mouth I warned them both that if the lady Baaltis consorts with any man not her husband duly named by her according to her right, she must die and her accomplice with her. Therefore, Aziel the Israelite, we give you to death, dooming you presently to be hurled from the edge of yonder precipice."

"I am in your power," said the prince proudly, "and you can murder if you will, because, forsooth, I have offended against some law of Baal, but I tell you, priest, that there are kings in Jerusalem and Egypt who will demand my blood at your hands. I have nothing more to say except to beseech you to spare the life of the lady Elissa, since the fault of the meeting was not hers, but mine."

"Prince," answered the Shadid gravely, "we know your rank and we know also that your blood will be required at our hands, but we who serve our gods, whose vengeance is so swift and terrible, cannot betray their law for the fear of any earthly kings. Yet, thus says this same law, it is not needful that you should die since for you there is a way of escape that leads to safety and great honour, and she who was the cause of your sin is the mistress of its gate. Elissa, holder of the spirit of Baaltis upon earth, if it be your pleasure to name this man husband before us all, then as the spouse of Baaltis he goes free, for he whom the Baaltis chooses cannot refuse her gift of love, but for so long as she shall live must rule with her as Shadid of El. But if you name him not, then as I have said, he must die, and now. Speak."

"It seems that my choice is small," said Elissa with a faint smile. "Praying you to pardon me for the deed, to save your life, prince Aziel, according to the ancient custom and privilege of the Baaltis, I name you consort and husband."

Now Aziel was about to answer her when the Shadid broke in hurriedly, "So be it," he said. "Lady, we hear your choice, and we accept it as we must, but not yet, prince Aziel, can you take your wife and with her my place and power. Your life is safe indeed, for since the Baaltis, being unwed, names you as her mate, you have done no sin. Yet she has sinned and doom awaits her, for against the law she has chosen as husband one who worships a strange god, and of all crimes that is the greatest. Therefore, either you must take incense and before us all make offering to El and Baaltis upon yonder altar, thus renouncing your faith and entering into ours, or she must die and you, your rank having passed from you with her breath, will be expelled from the city."

Now Aziel understood the trap that had been laid for him, and saw in it the handiwork of Sakon and Metem. Elissa having flagrantly violated the religious law, and he, being the cause of her crime, even the authority of the governor of the city could not prevent his daughter and his guest from being put upon their trial. Therefore, they had arranged this farce, for so it would seem to them, whereby both the offenders might escape the legal consequences of their offence, trusting, doubtless, to accident and the future to unravel this web of forced marriage, and to free Aziel from a priestly rank which he had not sought. It was only necessary that Elissa should formally choose him as her husband, and that Aziel should go through rite of throwing a few grains of incense upon an altar, and, the law satisfied, they would be both free and safe. What Metem, and those who worked with him, had forgotten was, that this offering of incense to Baal would be the most deadly of crimes in the eyes of any faithful Jew—one, indeed, which, were he alone concerned, he would die rather than commit.

When the prince heard this decree, and the full terror of the choice came home to his mind, his blood turned cold, and for a while his senses were bewildered. There was no escape for him; either he must abjure his faith at the price of his own soul, or, because of it, the woman whom he loved, now, before his eyes, must suffer a most horrible and sudden death. It was hideous to think of, and yet how could he do this sin in the face of heaven and of these ministers of Satan?

The moment was at hand; a priest held out to him a bowl of incense, a golden bowl, he noticed idly, with handles of green stone fashioned in the likeness of Baaltis, whose servant he was asked to declare himself. He, Aziel of the royal house of Israel, a servant of Baal and Baaltis, nay, a high-priest of their worship! It was monstrous, it might not be. But Elissa? Well, she must die—if this was not a farce, and in truth they meant to murder her; her life could not be bought at such a price.

"I cannot do it," he gasped with dry lips, thrusting aside the bowl.

Now all looked astonished, for his refusal had not been foreseen. There was a pause, and once more the woman Mesa, in her character of prosecutrix on behalf of the outraged gods, appeared before the altar, and said in her cold voice:

"The Jew whom the lady Baaltis has chosen as husband will not do homage to her gods. Therefore, as Mother of the priestesses and Advocate of Baaltis, I demand that Elissa, daughter of Sakon, be put to death, and the throne of Baaltis be purged of one who has defiled it, lest the swift and terrible vengeance of the goddess should fall upon this city."

The Shadid motioned to her to be silent, and addressed Aziel:—

"We pray you to think a while," he said, "before you give one to death whose only sin is that, being the high-priestess of our worship, she has named an unbeliever to fill the throne of El and be her husband. Out of pity for her fate we give you time to think."

Now Sakon, taking advantage of the pause, rushed forward, and throwing his arms about Aziel's knees, implored him in heart-breaking accents to preserve his only child from so horrible a doom. He said that did he refuse to save her because of his religious scruples, he would be a dog and a coward, and the scorn of all honest men for ever. It was for love of him that she had broken the priestly law, to violate which was death, and although he had been warned of her danger, yet in his wickedness and folly he had brought her to this pass. Would he then desert her now?

But Issachar thrust him aside, and broke in with fiery words:—

"Hearken not to this man, Aziel," he said, "who strives to work upon your weakness to the ruin of your soul. What! To save the life of one woman, whose fair face has brought so much trouble upon us all, would you deny your Lord and become the thrall of Baal and Ashtoreth? Let her die since die she must, and keep your own heart pure, for be assured, should you do otherwise, Jehovah, whom you renounce, will swiftly be avenged on you and her. At the beginning I warned you, and you would not listen. Now, Aziel, I warn you again, and woe! woe! woe! to you should you shut your ears to my message." Then lifting his hands towards the skies, he began to pray aloud that Aziel might be constant in his trial.

Meanwhile, Metem, who had drawn near, spoke in a low voice:—

"Prince," he said, "I am not chicken-hearted, and there are so many young women in the world that one more or less can scarcely matter; still, although she threatened to murder me three days ago, I cannot bear to see this one come to so dreadful a death. Prince, do not heed the howlings of that old fanatic, but remember that after all you are the cause of this lady's plight, and play the part of a man. Can you for the sake of your own scruples, however worthy, or of your own soul even, however valuable to yourself, doom the fair body of a woman who risked all for you to such an end as that?" And shuddering he nodded towards the gloomy precipice.

"Is there no other way?" Aziel asked him.

"None, I swear it. They did not wish to kill her, except that wild-cat Mesa who seeks her place, but having put her on her public trial, if you persist—they must.

"This is one of the few laws which cannot be broken for favour or for gold, since the people, who are already half-mad with fear of Ithobal, believe that to break it would bring the curses of heaven upon their city. Perhaps we might have found some other plan, but none of us even dreamed that you would refuse so small a thing for the sake of a woman whom you swore you loved."

"A small thing!" broke in Aziel.

"Yes, Prince, a very small thing. Remember, this offering of incense is but a form to which you are forced against your will—you can do penance for it afterwards when I have arranged for both of you to escape the city. If your God can be angry with you for burning a pinch of dust to save a woman, who at the least has dared much for you, then give me Baal, for he is less cruel."

Now Aziel looked towards him who held the bowl of incense. But Elissa who all this while had stood silent, stepped forward and spoke:—

"Prince Aziel," she said in a calm and quiet voice, "I named you husband to save your life, but with all my strength I pray of you, do not this thing to save mine, which is of little value and perhaps best ended. Remember, prince Aziel, that being what you are, a Jew, this act of offering, however small it seems, is yet the greatest of sins, and one with which you should not dare to stain your soul for the sake of a woman, who has chanced to love you to your sorrow. Be guided, therefore, by the true wisdom of Issachar and by my humble prayer. Make an end of your doubts and let me die, knowing that we do but part a while, since in the Gate of Death I shall wait for you, prince Aziel."

Before Aziel could answer, the Shadid, either because his patience was outworn, or because he wished to put him to a sharper trial, uttered a command. "Be it done to her as she desires."

Thereon four priests seized Elissa by the wrists and ankles. Carrying her to the edge of the precipice, they thrust her back till she hung over it, her long hair streaming downwards, and the red light of the sunset shining upon her upturned ghastly face. Then they paused, waiting for the signal to let her go. The Shadid raised his wand and said:—

"Is it your pleasure that this woman should die or live, prince Aziel? Decide swiftly, for my arm is weak, and when the wand falls opportunity for choice will have passed from you."

Now all eyes were fixed upon the wand, and the intense silence was only broken by Sakon's cry of despair. Metem wrung his hands in grief; even Issachar veiled his eyes with his robe, to shut out the sight of dread, and the priest, who bore the bowl of incense, thrust it towards Aziel imploringly.

For some seconds, three perhaps, though to him they seemed an age, the heart of Aziel was racked and torn in this terrific contest. Then he glanced at the agonized face of the doomed woman, and just as the wand began to bend, his human love and pity conquered.

"May He Whom I blaspheme forgive me," he murmured, adding aloud, "I will do sacrifice." Taking the incense in his hand now he cast it into the flames upon the altar, repeating mechanically after the Shadid: "By this sacrifice and homage, body and soul I give myself to you and worship you, El and Baaltis, the only true gods."

The echo of Aziel's voice died away, and the fumes of the incense rose in a straight dense column upon that quiet air. To his tormented mind, it seemed as though its smoke took the form of an avenging angel, holding in the hand a sword of flame, wherewith to drive away his perjured soul from Heaven, as our first forefathers were driven from the shining gates of paradise. Yes, and they were not human, those spectators who, in the intense glow of the sunset, stood in their still ranks and stared at him with wide and eager eyes. Surely they were fiends red with the blood of men, fiends gathered from the Pit to bear everlasting witness to the unpardonable sin of his apostasy.

Chapter XIV

The Martyrdom of Issachar

It was done, and from the mouths of the circle of priests and priestesses leapt a shrill and sudden cry of triumph. For had not their gods conquered? Had not this high-placed servant of the hated Lord of Israel been caught by the bait of a priestess of Baaltis, and seduced by her distress to deny and reject Him? Was not evil once more triumphant, and must not they, its ministers, rejoice?

Again the Shadid raised his wand and they were silent.

"Brother you have, indeed, done well and wisely," he said, addressing Aziel. "Now take to wife the divine lady who has chosen you," and he pointed to Elissa, who lay prostrated on the rock. "Yes, take her and be happy in her love, sitting in my seat, which henceforth is yours, as ruler of the priests of El and master of their mysteries, forgetting the follies of your former faith, and spitting on its altars. Hail to you, Shadid, Lord of the Baaltis and chosen of El! Take him, you priests, and with him the divine lady, his wife, to bear them in triumph to their high house."

"What of the Levite?" asked the woman Mesa.

The Shadid glanced at Issachar, who all this while had stood like one stricken to the soul, woe stamped upon his face, and a stare of horror in his eyes. "Jew," he said, "I had forgotten you, but you also are on your trial, who dared against the law to hold secret meeting with the lady Baaltis. For this sin the punishment is death, nor, as I think, would any woman name you husband to save you. Still in this hour of joy we will be merciful; therefore do as your master did, cast incense on the altar, uttering the appointed words, and go your way."

"Before I make my offering on yonder altar according to your command, I have indeed some words to say, O priest of El," answered Issachar quietly, but in a voice that chilled the blood of those who listened.

"First, I address myself to you, Aziel, and to you, woman," and he pointed to Elissa, who had risen, and leaned, trembling, upon her father. "My dream is fulfilled. Aziel, you have sinned indeed, and must bear the appointed punishment of your sin. Yet hear a message of mercy spoken through my lips: Because you have sinned through love and pity, your offence is not unto death. Still shall you sorrow for it all your life's days, and in desolation of heart and bitterness of soul shall creep back to the feet of Him you have forsworn.

"Woman, your spirit is noble and your feet are set in the way of righteousness, yet through you has this offence come. Therefore your love shall bear no fruit, nor shall the blasphemy of your beloved save your flesh from doom. Upon this earth there is no hope for you, daughter of Sakon; set your eyes beyond it, for there alone is hope.

"Yonder she stands who swore our lives away?" and he fixed his burning gaze on Mesa. "Priestess, you plotted this that you might succeed to the throne of Baaltis; now hear your fate: You shall live to sweep the huts and bear the babes of savages. You, priest," and he pointed to the Shadid, "I read your heart;

you design to murder this apostate whom you greet as your successor that you may usurp his place. I show you yours: it lies in the bellies of the jackals of the desert.

"For you priests and priestesses of El and Baaltis, think of my words, and raise the loud song of triumph to your gods when you yourselves are their offering, and the red flame of the fire burns you up, all of you save your sins, which are immortal. O citizens of an accursed city, look on the hill-top yonder and tell me, what do you see in the light of the dying day? A sheen of spears, is it not? They draw near to your hearts, you whose day is done indeed, citizens of an accursed city whereof the very name shall be forgotten, and the naked towers shall become but a source of wonder to men unborn.

"And now, O priest, having said my say, as you bid me, I make my offering upon your altar."

Then, while all stood fearful and amazed, Issachar the Levite sprang forward, and seizing the ancient image of Baaltis, he spat upon it and dashed the priceless consecrated thing down upon the altar, where it broke into fragments, and was burned with the fire.

"My offering is made," he said; "may He whom I serve accept it. Now after the offering comes the sacrifice; son Aziel, fare you well."

For a few moments a silence of horror and dismay fell upon the assembly as they gazed at the shattered and burning fragments of their holy image. Then moved by a common impulse, with curses and yells of fury, the priests and priestesses sprang from their seats and hurled themselves upon Issachar, who stood awaiting them with folded arms. They smote him with their ivory rods, they rent and tore him with their hands and teeth, worrying him as dogs worry a fox of the hills, till at length the life was beaten and trampled out of him and he lay dead.

Thus terribly, but yet by such a death of martyrdom as he would have chosen, perished Issachar the Levite.

Unarmed though he was, Aziel had sprung to his aid, but Metem and Sakon, knowing that he would but bring about his own destruction, flung themselves upon him and held him back. Whilst he was still struggling with them the end came, and Issachar grew still for ever. Then, as the sun sank and the darkness fell, Aziel's strength left him, and presently he slipped to the ground senseless.

Thereafter it seemed to Aziel that he was plunged in an endless and dreadful dream, and that through its turmoil and shifting visions, he could see continually the dreadful death of Issachar, and hear his stern accents prophesying woe to him who renounces the God of his forefathers to bow the knee to Baal.

At length he awoke from that horror-haunted sleep to find himself lying in a strange chamber. It was night, and lamps burned in the chamber, and by their light he saw a man whose face he knew mixing a draught in a glass phial. So weak was he that at first he could not remember the man's name, then by slow degrees it came to him.

"Metem," he said, "where am I?"

The Phoenician looked up from his task, smiled, and answered:—

"Where you should be, Prince, in your own house, the palace of the Shadid. But you must not speak, for you have been ill; drink this and sleep."

Aziel swallowed the draught and was instantly overcome by slumber. When he awoke the sun was shining brightly through the window place, and its rays fell upon the shrewd, kindly face of Metem, who, seated on a stool, watched him, his chin resting in his hand.

"Tell me all that has befallen, friend," said Aziel presently, "since—" and he shuddered.

"Since you were married after a new fashion and that bigoted but most honourable fool, Issachar, went to his reward. Well, I will when you have eaten," answered Metem as he gave him food. "First," he said, after a while, "you have lain here for three days raving in a fever, nursed by myself and visited by your wife the lady Baaltis, whenever she could escape from her religious duties—"

"Elissa! Has she been here?" asked Aziel.

"Calm yourself, Prince, certainly she has, and, what is more, she will be back soon. Secondly: Ithobal has been as good as his word, and invests the city with a vast army, cutting off all supplies and possibilities of escape. It is believed that he will try an assault within the next week, which many think may be successful. Thirdly: to avoid this risk it is rumoured that the priests and priestesses, at the instance of the council, are discussing the wisdom of giving over to the king the person of the daughter of Sakon. This, it is said, could be done on the plea that her election as the lady Baaltis was brought about with bribery, and is, therefore, void, as she was not chosen by the pure and unassisted will of the goddess."

"But," said Aziel, "she is my wife according to their religious law; how then can she be given in marriage to another?"

"Nay, Prince, if she is not the lady Baaltis your husbandship falls to the ground with the rest, for you are not the Shadid, an office with which perchance you can dispense. But all this priestly juggling means little, the truth being that the city in its terror is ready to throw her—or for the matter of that, Baaltis herself if they could lay hands on her—as a sop to Ithobal, hoping thereby to appease his rage. The lady Elissa knows her danger—but here she comes to speak for herself."

As he spoke the curtains at the end of the chamber were drawn, and through them came Elissa, clad in her splendid robes of office and wearing upon her brow the golden crescent of the moon.

"How goes it with the prince, Metem?" she asked in her soft voice, glancing anxiously towards the couch which was half-hidden in the shadow of the wall.

"Look for yourself, lady," answered the Phoenician bowing before her.

"Elissa, Elissa!" cried Aziel, raising himself and opening his arms.

She saw and heard, then, with a low cry, she ran swiftly to him and was wrapped in his embrace. Thus they stayed a while, murmuring words of love and greeting.

"Is it your pleasure that I should leave you?" asked Metem presently. "No? Then, Prince, I would have you remember that you are still very weak and should not give way to violent emotions."

"Listen, Aziel," said Elissa, untwining his arms from about her neck, "there is no time for tenderness; moreover, you should show none to one who, in name at least, is still the high-priestess of Baaltis, though in truth she worships her no longer. It was noble of you indeed to offer incense upon the altar of El that my life might be saved. But when I prayed you not, I spoke from the heart, and bitterly, bitterly do I grieve that for my sake you should have stained your hands with such a sin. Moreover, it will avail nothing, for the doom of the prophet Issachar lies upon us, and I cannot escape from death, neither can you escape remorse, and as I think, that worst of all desires—the desire for the dead."

"Can we not still flee the city?" asked Aziel.

"Metem will tell you that it is impossible; day and night I am watched and guarded, yes, Mesa dogs me from door to door. Also Ithobal holds Zimboe so firmly in his net that no sparrow could fly out of it and he not know. And there is worse to tell: Beloved, they purpose to give me up as a peace-offering to Ithobal. Yes, even my father is of the plot, for in his despair he thinks it his duty to sacrifice his daughter to save the town, if, indeed, that will suffice to save us."

"But you are the Baaltis and inviolate."

"In such a time the goddess herself would not be held inviolate in Zimboe, much less her priestess, Aziel. I have discovered that this very night they have laid their plans to seize me. Mesa and others have been chosen for the deed, and afterwards they think to offer me as a bribe to Ithobal, who will take no other price."

Aziel groaned aloud: "It were better that we should die," he said.

She nodded and answered: "It were better that I should die. But hear me, for I also have a plan, and there is still hope, though very little. Perhaps, as you drew near to Zimboe by the coast road, you may have noted three miles or more from the gates of the city, and almost overhanging the path on which you travelled, a shoulder of the mountain where the rock is cut away, showing the narrow entrance to a cave closed with a gate of bronze?"

"I saw it," answered Aziel, "and was told that there was the most sacred burying-place of the city."

"It is the tomb of the high-priestesses of Baaltis," went on Elissa, "and this day at sunset I must visit it to lay an offering upon the shrine of her who was the Baaltis before me, entering alone, and closing the gate, for it is not lawful that any one should pass in there with me. Now, the plan is to lay hands on me as I go back from the tomb to the palace—but I shall not go back. Aziel, I shall stay in the tomb—nay, do not fear—not dead. I have hidden food and water there, enough for many days, and there with the departed I shall live —till I am of their number."

"But if so, how can it help you, Elissa, for they will break in the gates of the place, and drag you away?"

"Then, Aziel, they will drag away a corpse, and that they will scarcely care to present to Ithobal. See, I have hidden poison in my breast, and here at my girdle hangs a dagger; are not the two of them enough to make an end of one frail life? Should they dare to touch me, I shall tell them through the bars that most certainly I shall drink the bane, or use the knife; and when they know it, they will leave me unharmed, hoping to starve me out, or trusting to chance to snare me living."

"You are bold," murmured Aziel in admiration, "but self-murder is a sin."

"It is a sin that I will dare, beloved, as in past days I would have dared it for less cause, rather than be given alive into the hands of Ithobal; for to whoever else I may be false, to you through life and death I will be true."

Now Aziel groaned in his doubt and bitterness of heart; then turning to Metem, he asked:—

"Have you anything to say, Metem?"

"Yes, Prince, two things," answered the Phoenician. "First, that the lady Elissa is rash, indeed, to speak so openly before me who might carry her words to the council or the priests."

"Nay, Metem, I am not rash, for I know that, although you love money, you will not betray me."

"You are right, lady, I shall not, for money would be of little service to me in a city that is about to be taken by storm. Also I hate Ithobal, who threatened my life—as you did also, by the way—and will do my best to keep you from his clutches. Now for my second point: it is that I can see little use in all this because Ithobal, being defrauded of you, will attack, and then—"

"And then he may be beaten, Metem, for the citizens will at any rate fight for their lives, and the Prince Aziel here, who is a general skilled in war, will fight also if he has recovered strength—"

"Do not fear, Elissa; give me two days, and I will fight to the death," said Aziel.

"At the least," she went on, "this scheme gives us breathing time, and who knows but that fortune will turn. Or if it does not, since it is impossible for me to escape from the city, I have no better."

"No more have I," said Metem, "for at length the oldest fox comes to his last double. I could escape from this city, or the prince might escape, or the lady Elissa even might possibly escape disguised, but I am sure that all three of us could not escape, seeing that within the walls we are watched and without them the armies of Ithobal await us. Oh! prince Aziel, I should have done well to go, as I might have gone when you and Issachar were taken after that mad meeting in the temple, from which I never looked for anything but ill; but I grow foolish in my old age, and thought that I should like to see the last of you. Well, so far we are all alive, except Issachar, who, although bigoted, was still the most worthy of us, but how long we shall remain alive I cannot say.

"Now our best chance is to defeat Ithobal if we can, and afterwards in the confusion to fly from Zimboe and join our servants, to whom I have sent word to await us in a secret place beyond the first range of hills. If we cannot—why then we must go a little sooner than we expected to find out who it is that really shapes the destinies of men, and whether or no the sun and moon are the chariots of El and Baaltis. But, Prince, you turn pale."

"It is nothing," said Aziel, "bring me some water, the fever still burns in me."

Metem went to seek for water, while Elissa knelt by the couch and pressed her lover's hand.

"I dare stay no longer," she whispered, "and Aziel, I know not how or when we shall meet again, but my heart is heavy, for, alas! I think that doom draws near me. I have brought much sorrow upon you, Aziel, and yet more upon myself, and I have given you nothing, except that most common of all things, a woman's love."

"That most perfect of all things," he answered, "which I am glad to have lived to win."

"Yes, but not at the price that you have paid for it. I know well what it must have cost you to cast that incense on the flame, and I pray to your God, who has become my God, to visit the sin of it on my head and to leave yours unharmed. Aziel, Aziel! woman or spirit, while I have life and memory, I am yours, and yours only; clean-handed I leave you, and if we may meet again in this or in any other world, clean and faithful I shall come to you again. Glad am I to have lived, because in my life I have known you and you have sworn you love me. Glad shall I be to live again if again I may know you and hear that oath—if not, it is sleep I seek; for life without you to me would be a hell. You grow weak, and I must go. Farewell, and living or dead, forget me not; swear that you will not forget me."

"I swear it," he answered faintly; "and Heaven grant that I may die for you, not you for me."

"That is no prayer of mine," she whispered; and, bending, kissed him on the brow, for he was too weak to lift his lips to hers.

Then she was gone.

Chapter XV

Elissa Takes Sanctuary

Two more hours had passed, and in the evening light a procession of priestesses might be seen advancing slowly towards the holy tomb along a narrow road of rock cut in the mountain face. In front of this procession, wearing a black veil over her broidered robes, walked Elissa with downcast eyes and hair unbound in token of grief, while behind her came Mesa and other priestesses bearing in bowls of alabaster the offerings to the dead, food and wine, and lamps of oil, and vases filled with perfumes. Behind these again marched the mourners, women who sang a funeral dirge and from time to time broke into a wail of simulated grief. Nor, indeed, was their woe as hollow as might be thought, since from that mountain path they could see the outposts of the army of Ithobal upon the plain, and note with a shudder of fear the spear-heads of his countless thousands shining in the gorges of the opposing heights. It was not for the dead Baaltis that they mourned this day, but for the fate which overshadowed them and their city of gold.

"May the curse of all the gods fall on her," muttered one of the priestesses as she toiled forward beneath her load of offerings; "because she is beautiful and pettish, we must be put to the spear, or become the wives of savages," and she pointed with her chin to Elissa, who walked in front, lost in her own thoughts.

"Have patience," answered Mesa at her side, "you know the plan— to-night that proud girl and false priestess shall sleep in the camp of Ithobal."

"Will he be satisfied with that," asked the woman, "and leave the city in peace?"

"They say so," answered Mesa with a laugh, "though it is strange that a king should exchange spoil and glory for one round-eyed, thin-limbed girl who loves his rival. Well, let us thank the gods that made men foolish, and gave us women wit to profit by their folly. If he wants her, let him take her, for few will be poorer by her loss."

"You at least will be richer," said the other woman, "and by the crown of Baaltis. Well, I do not grudge it you, and as for the daughter of Sakon, she shall be Ithobal's if I take her to him limb by limb."

"Nay, sister, that is not the bargain; remember she must be delivered to him without hurt or blemish; otherwise we shall do sacrilege in vain. Be silent, here is the cave."

Reaching the platform in front of the tomb, the procession of mourners ranged themselves about it in a semi-circle. They stood with their backs to the edge of a cliff that rose sheer for sixty feet or more from the plain beneath, across which, but at a little distance from the foot of the precipice ran the road followed by the caravans of merchants in their journeys to and from the coast. Then, a hymn having been sung invoking the blessing of the gods on the dead priestess, Elissa, as the Baaltis, unlocked the gates of bronze with a golden key that hung at her girdle, and the bearers of the bowls of offerings pushed them into the mouth of the tomb, whose threshold they were not allowed to pass. Next, with bowed heads and hands crossed upon her breast, Elissa entered the tomb, and locking the bronze gate behind her, took up two of the bowls and vanished with them into its gloomy depths.

"Why did she lock the gates?" asked a priestess of Mesa. "It is not customary."

"Doubtless because it was her pleasure to do so," answered Mesa sharply, though she also wondered why Elissa had locked the gate.

When an hour was gone by and Elissa had not returned, her wonder turned to fear and doubt.

"Call to the lady Baaltis," she said, "for her prayers are long, and I fear lest she should have come to harm."

So they called, setting heir lips against the bars of the gate till presently, Elissa, holding a lamp in her hand, came and stood before them.

"Why do you disturb me in the sanctuary?" she asked.

"Lady, because they set the night watch on the walls," answered Mesa, "and it is time to return to the temple."

"Return then," said Elissa, "and leave me in peace. What, you cannot, Mesa? Nay, and shall I tell you why? Because you had plotted to deliver me this night to those who should lead me as a peace-offering to Ithobal, and when you come to them empty-handed they will greet you with harsh words. Nay, do not trouble to deny it, Mesa. I also have my spies, and know all the plan; and, therefore, I have taken sanctuary in this holy place."

Now Mesa pressed her thin lips together and answered:—

"Those who dare to lay hands upon the person of the living Baaltis will not shrink from seeking her in the company of her dead sisters."

"I know it, Mesa; but the gates are barred, and here I have food and drink in plenty."

"Gates, however strong, can be broken," answered the priestess, "so, lady, do not wait till you are dragged hence like some discovered slave."

"Ay," replied Elissa, with a little laugh, "but what if rather than be thus dishonoured, I should choose to break another gate, that of my own life? Look, traitress, here is poison and here is bronze, and I swear to you that should any lay a hand upon me, by one or other of them I will die before their eyes. Then, if you will, bear these bones to Ithobal and take his thanks for them. Now, begone, and give this message to my father and to all those who have plotted with him, that since they cannot bribe Ithobal with my beauty, they will do well to be men, and to fight him with their swords."

Then she turned and left them, vanishing into the darkness of the tomb.

Great indeed was the dismay of the councillors of Zimboe and of the priests who had plotted with them when, an hour later, Mesa came, not to deliver Elissa into their hands, but to repeat to them her threats and message. In vain did they appeal to Sakon, who only shook his head and answered:—

"Of this I am sure, that what my daughter has threatened that she will certainly do if you force her to the choice. But if you will not believe me, go ask her and satisfy yourselves. I know well what she will answer you, and I hold that this is a judgment upon us, who first made her Baaltis against her will, then threatened her with death because of the prince Aziel, and now would do sacrilege to her sacred office and violence to herself by tearing her from her consecrated throne, breaking her bond of marriage and delivering her to Ithobal."

So the leaders of the councillors visited the holy tomb and reasoned with Elissa through the bars. But they got no comfort from her, for she spoke to them with the phial of poison in her bosom and the naked dagger in her hand, telling them what she had told Mesa—that they had best give up their plottings and fight Ithobal like men, seeing that even if she surrendered herself to him, when he grew weary of her the war must come at last.

"For a hundred years," she added, "this storm has gathered, and now it must burst. When it has rolled away it will be known who is master of the land—the ancient city of Zimboe, or Ithobal king of the Tribes."

So they went back as they had come, and next day at the dawn, with a bold face but heavy hearts, received the messengers of king Ithobal, and told them their tale. The messengers heard and laughed.

"We are glad," they answered, "since we, who are not in love with the daughter of Sakon, desire war and not peace, holding as we do that the time has come when you upstart white men—you outlanders—who have usurped our country to suck away its wealth should be set beneath our heel. Nor do we think that the task will be difficult for surely we have little to fear from a city of low money seekers whose councillors cannot even conquer the will of a single maid."

Then in their despair the elders offered other girls to Ithobal in marriage, as many as he would, and with them a great bribe in money. But the envoys took their leave, saying that nothing would avail since they preferred spear-thrusts to gold, for which they had little use, and Ithobal, their king, had fixed his fancy on one woman alone.

So with a heavy and foreboding heart, the city of Zimboe prepared itself to resist attack, for as they had guessed, when he learned all, the rage of Ithobal was great. Nor would he listen to any terms that they could offer save one which they had no power to grant—that Elissa should be delivered unharmed into his hands. Councils of war were held, and to these, so soon as he was sufficiently recovered from his sickness, the prince Aziel was bidden, for he was known to be a skilled captain; therefore, though he had been the cause of much of their trouble, they sought his aid. Also, should the struggle be prolonged, they hoped through him to win Israel, and perhaps Egypt, to their cause.

Aziel's counsel was that they should sally out against the army of Ithobal by night, since he expected to attack and not to be attacked, but to that advice they would not listen, for they trusted to their walls. Indeed, in this Metem supported them, and when the prince argued with him, he answered:—

"Your tactics would be good enough, Prince, if you had at your back the lions of Judah, or the wild Arab horsemen of the desert. But here you must deal with men of my own breed, and we Phoenicians are traders, not fighting men. Like rats, we fight only when there is no other chance for our lives; nor do we strike the first blow. It is true that there are some good soldiers in the city, but they are foreign mercenaries; and as for the rest, half-breeds and freed slaves, they belong as much to Ithobal as to Sakon, and are not to be trusted. No, no; let us stay behind our walls, for they at least were built when men were honest and will not betray us."

Now in Zimboe were three lines of defence; first, that of a single wall built about the huts of the slaves upon the plain, then that of a double wall of stone with a ditch between thrown round the Phoenician city, and lastly, the great fortress-temple and the rocky heights above. These, guarded as they were by many strongholds within whose circle the cattle were herded, as it was thought, could only be taken with the sword of hunger.

At last the storm burst, for on the fifth morning after Elissa had barred herself within the tomb, Ithobal attacked the native town. Uttering their wild battle-cries, tens of thousands of his savage warriors, armed with great spears and shields of ox-hide, and wearing crests of plumes upon their heads, charged down upon the outer wall. Twice they were driven back, but the work was in bad repair and too long to defend, so that at the third rush they flowed over it like lines of marching ants, driving its defenders before them to the inner gates. In this battle some were killed, but the most of the slaves threw down their arms and went over to Ithobal, who spared them, together with their wives and children.

Through all the night that followed, the generals of Zimboe made ready for the onslaught which must come. Everywhere within the circuit of the inner wall troops were stationed, while the double southern gateway, where prince Aziel was the captain in command, was built up with loose blocks of stone.

A while before the dawn, just as the eastern sky grew grey, Aziel, watching from his post above the gate of the wall, heard the fierce war-song of the Tribes swell suddenly from fifty thousand throats and the measured tramp of their innumerable feet. Then the day broke, and he saw them advancing in three armies towards the three points chosen for attack, the largest of the armies, headed by Ithobal the king, directing its march upon the walled gate of which he was in command.

It was a wondrous and a fearful sight, that of these hordes of plumed warriors, their broad spears flashing in the sunrise, and their fierce faces alight with hereditary hate and the lust of slaughter. Never had Aziel seen such a spectacle, nor could he look upon it without dreading the issue of the war, for if they were savages, these foes were brave as the lions of their own plains, and had sworn by the head of their king to drag down the sheltering walls of Zimboe with their naked hands, or die to the last man.

Turning his head with a sigh of doubt, Aziel found Metem standing at his side.

"Have you seen her?" he asked eagerly.

"No, Prince. How could I see her at night when she sits in a tomb like a fox in his burrow? But I have heard her."

"What did she say? Quick man, tell me."

"But little, Prince, for the tomb is watched and I dared not stay there long. She sent you her greetings and would have you know that her heart will be with you in the battle, and her prayers beseech the throne of Heaven for your safety. Also she said that she is well, though it is lonesome there in the grave among the bodies of the dead priestesses of Baaltis whose spirits, as she vows, haunt her dreams, reviling her because she desecrates their sepulchre and has renounced their god."

"Lonesome, indeed," said Aziel with a shudder; "but tell me, Metem, had she no other word?"

"Yes, Prince, but not of good omen, for now as always she is sure that her doom is at hand, and that you two will meet no more. Still she bade me tell you that all your life long her spirit shall companion you though it be unseen, to receive you at the last on the threshold of the underworld."

Aziel turned his head away, and said presently:—

"If that be so, may it receive me soon."

"Have no fear, Prince," replied Metem with a grim laugh, "look yonder," and he pointed to the advancing hosts.

"These walls are strong and we shall beat them back," said Aziel.

"Nay, Prince, for strong walls do not avail without strong hearts to guard them, and those of the womanish citizens of Zimboe and their hired soldiers are white with fear. I tell you that the prophecies of Issachar the Levite, made yonder in the temple on the day of the sacrifice, and again in the hour of his death, have taken hold of the people, and by eating out their valour, fulfil themselves.

"Men hint at them, the women whisper them in closets, and the very children cry them in the streets.

"More—one man last night pointed to the skies and shrieked that in them he saw that fiery sword of doom of which the prophet spoke hanging point downwards above the city, whereon all present vowed they saw it too, though, as I think, it was but a cross of stars. Another tells how that he met the very spirit of Issachar stalking through the market-place, and that peering into the eyes of the wraith, as in a mirror, he saw a great flame wrapping the temple walls, and by the light of it his own dead body. This man was the priest who first struck down the holy Levite yonder in the place of judgment.

"Again, when the lady Mesa did sacrifice last night on behalf of the Baaltis who has fled, the child they offered, an infant of six months, stirred on the altar after it was dead and cried with a loud voice that before three suns had set, its blood should be required at their hands. That is the story, and if I do not believe it, this at least is true, that the priestesses fled fast from the secret chamber of death, for I met them as they ran shrieking in their terror and tearing at their robes. But what need is there to dwell on omens, true or false, when cowards man the walls, and the spears of Ithobal shine yonder like all the stars of heaven? Prince, I tell you that this ancient city is doomed, and in it, as I fear, we must end our wanderings upon earth."

"So be it, if it must be," answered Aziel, "at the least I will die fighting."

"And I also will die fighting, Prince, not because I love it, but because it is better than being butchered in cold blood by a savage with a spear. Oh! why did you ever chance to stumble upon the lady Elissa making her prayer to Baaltis, and what evil spirit was it which filled your brains with this sudden madness of love towards each other? That was the beginning of the trouble, which, but for those eyes of hers, would have held off long enough to see us safe at Tyre, though doubtless soon or late it must have come. But see, yonder marches Ithobal at the head of his guard. Give me a bow, the flight is long, but perchance I can reach his black heart with an arrow."

"Save your strength," answered Aziel, "the range is too great, and presently you will have enough of shooting," and he turned to talk to the officers of the guard.

Chapter XVI

The Cage of Death

An hour later the attack commenced at chosen points of the double wall, one of them being the southern gate. In front of the advancing columns of savages were driven vast numbers of slaves, many of whom had been captured, or had surrendered in the outer town. These men were laden with faggots to fill the ditch, rude ladders wherewith to scale the walls, and heavy trunks of trees to be used in breaching them. For the most part, they were unarmed, and protected only by their burdens, which they held before them as shields, and by the arrows of the warriors of Ithobal. But these did little harm to the defenders, who were hidden behind the walls, whereas the shafts of the garrison, rained on them from above, killed or wounded the slaves by scores, who, poor creatures, when they turned to fly, were driven onward by the spear-points of the savages, to be slain in heaps like game in a pitfall. Still, some of them lived, and running under the shelter of the wall, began to breach it with the rude battering rams, and to raise the scaling ladders till death found them, or they were worn out with excitement, fear and labour.

Then the real attack began. With fierce yells, the threefold column rushed at the wall, and began to work the rams and scale the ladders, while the defenders above showered spears and arrows upon them, or crushed them with heavy stones, or poured upon their heads boiling pitch and water, heated in great cauldrons which stood at hand.

Time after time they were driven back with heavy loss; and, time upon time, fresh hordes of them advanced to the onslaught. Thrice, at the southern gate, were the ladders raised, and thrice the stormers appeared above the level of the wall, to be hurled back, crushed and bleeding, to the earth beneath.

Thus the long day wore on and still the defenders held their own.

"We shall win," shouted Aziel to Metem, as a fresh ladder was cast down with its weight of men to the death-strewn plain.

"Yes, here we shall win because we fight," answered the Phoenician, "but elsewhere it may be otherwise." Indeed for a while the attack upon the south gate slackened.

Another hour passed and presently to the left of them rose a wild yell of triumph, and with it a shout of "Fly to the second wall. The foe is in the fosse!"

Metem looked and there, down the great ditch, 300 paces to their left, a flood of savages poured towards them. "Come," he said, "the outer wall is lost." But as he spoke once more the ladders rose against the gates and flanking towers and once more Aziel sprang to cast them down. When the deed was done, he looked behind him to find that he was cut off and surrounded. Metem and most of his men indeed had gained the inner wall in safety, while he with twelve only of his bravest soldiers, Jews of his own following, who had stayed to help him to throw back the ladders, were left upon the gateway tower. Nor was escape any longer possible, for both the plain without and the fosse within were filled with the men of Ithobal who advanced also by hundreds down the broad coping of the captured wall.

"Now there is but one thing that we can do," said Aziel; "fight bravely till we are slain."

As he spoke a javelin cast from the wall beneath struck him upon the breastplate, and though the bronze turned the iron point, it brought him to his knees. When he found his feet again, he heard a voice calling him by name, and looking down, saw Ithobal clad in golden harness and surrounded by his captains.

"You cannot escape, prince Aziel," cried the king; "yield now to my mercy."

Aziel heard, and setting an arrow to his bow, loosed it at Ithobal beneath. He was a strong and skilful archer, and the heavy shaft pierced the golden helmet of the king, cutting his scalp down to the bone.

"That is my answer," cried Aziel, as Ithobal rolled upon the ground beneath the shock of the blow. But very soon the king was up and crying his commands from behind the shield-hedge of his captains.

"Let the prince Aziel, and the Jews with him, be taken alive and brought to me," he shouted. "I will give a great reward in cattle to those who capture them unharmed; but if any do them hurt, they themselves shall be put to death."

The captains bowed and issued their orders, and presently Aziel and his companions saw lines of unarmed men creeping up ladders set at every side of the lofty tower. Again and again they cast off the ladders, till at length, being so few, they could stir them no more because of the weight upon them, but must hack at the heads of the stormers as they appeared above the parapet, killing them one by one.

In this fashion they slew many, but their arms grew weary at last, and ever under the eye of their king, the brave savages crept upward, heedless of death, till, with a shout, they poured over the battlements and rushed at the little band of Jews.

Now rather than be taken, Aziel sought to throw himself from the tower, but his companions held him, and thus at last it came about that he was seized and bound.

As they dragged him to the stairway he looked across the fosse and saw the mercenaries flying from the inner wall, although it was still unbreached, and saw the citizens of Zimboe streaming by thousands to the narrow gateway of the temple fortress.

Then Aziel groaned in his heart and struggled no more, for he knew that the fate of the ancient town was sealed, and that the prophecy of Issachar would be fulfilled.

A while later Aziel and those with him, their hands bound behind their backs, were led by hide ropes tied about their necks through the army of the Tribes that jeered and spat upon them as they passed, to a tent of sewn hides on the plain, above which floated the banner of Ithobal. Into this tent the prince was thrust alone, and there forced upon his knees by the soldiers who held him. Before him upon a couch covered with a lion skin lay the great shape of Ithobal, while physicians washed his wounded scalp.

"Greeting, son of Israel and Pharaoh," he said in a mocking voice; "truly you are wise thus to do homage to the king of the world."

"A poor jest," answered Aziel, glancing at those who held him down; "true homage is of the heart, king Ithobal."

"I know it, Jew, and this also you shall give me when you are humbler. Who taught you the use of the bow? You shoot well," and he pointed to his blood-stained helm, which was still transfixed by the arrow.

"Nay," answered Aziel, "I shot but ill, for my arm was weary. When next I draw a string against your breast, king Ithobal, I promise you a straighter shaft."

"Well said," answered the king with a laugh, "but know, dog of a Jew, that now it is my turn to draw the string—how, I will show you afterwards. Have they told you that the city has fallen, and that my captains hold the gates, while the cowards of Zimboe are penned like sheep within the temple and on the cliff-edged height above? They have fled hither for safety, but I tell you that they would be more safe on yonder plain, for I have the key of their stronghold, a certain passage leading from the palace of the Baaltis to the temple; you know if it, I think. Yes, and if I had not, very soon hunger and thirst would work for me.

"Well, Jew, I have won, and with less trouble than I thought, and now I hold the great city in hostage, to save or to destroy as it shall please me, though that arrow of yours went near to robbing me of my crown of victory."

"So be it," answered Aziel, indifferently; "I have played my part, now things must go as Fate may will."

"Yes, Jew, you fought well till they deserted you, and the doom of cowards is little to a brave man. But what of the lady Elissa? Nay, I know all; she has taken refuge in the tomb of Baaltis, has she not, with poison in her bosom and bronze at her girdle to be used against her own life, should they lay hands on her or give her to me? And all this she does for the love of you, prince Aziel; for the love of you she refuses to become my queen, ruling over that city which I have conquered, and all my unnumbered tribes.

"Do you guess now why I caused you to be taken living? I will tell you; that you may be the bait to draw her to me. To kill you would be easy; but how would that serve, seeing that then she herself would choose to die? But, perchance, to save your life she will live also— yes, and give herself to me. At least, I will try it; should the plan fail—then you can pay the price of her pride with your blood, prince Aziel."

"That I would do gladly," answered Aziel, "but oh! what a cross-bred hound you are who thus can seek to torture the heart of a helpless woman! Have you then no manhood that you can stoop to such a coward's plot?"

"Fool! it is because of my manhood that I do stoop to it," said Ithobal angrily. "Doubtless you think that a mad fancy and naught else drives me to the deed, but it is not so, although in truth my heart— like yours—chooses this woman to be my wife and none other. That fondness I might conquer, but look you, of all things living this lady alone has dared to cross my will, so that to-day even the sentries on their rounds and the savage women in the kraals tell each other of how Ithobal, the great king of an hundred tribes, has been baffled and mocked at by a girl who despises him because his blood is not all white. Thus I am become a laughing-stock, and therefore I will win her, cost me what it may."

"And I, king Ithobal, tell you that you will not win her—no, not if you torture me to death before her eyes."

"That we shall see," said the king with a sneer. Then he called to his guard and added, "Let this man and his companions be taken to the place prepared for them."

Now Aziel was dragged from the tent and thrust into a wooden cage, such as were used for carrying slaves and women from place to place upon the backs of camels. His soldiers, who had been taken with him, were thrust also into cages, and, with himself laden upon camels that were waiting, two cages to each camel. Then a cloth was thrown over them, and, rising to their feet, the camels began to march.

When they had covered a league or more of ground Aziel learned from the motion of the camel upon which he was secured, and the sound of the repeated blows of its drivers, that they were ascending some steep place. At length they reached the top of it, and were unloaded from the beasts like merchandise, but he could see nothing, for by now the night had fallen. Then, still in the cages, they were carried to a tent, where food and water were given them through the bars, after which, so weary was Aziel with war, misery and the remains of recent illness, that he fell asleep.

At daybreak he awoke, or rather was awakened, by the sound of a familiar voice, and, looking through his bars, perceived Metem standing before them, guarded but unbound, with indignation written on his face, and tears in his quick eyes.

"Alas!" he cried, "that I should have lived to see the seed of Israel and Pharaoh thus fastened like a wild beast in a den, while barbarians make a mock of him. Oh! Prince, it were better that you should die rather than endure such shame."

"Misfortunes are the master of man, not man of his misfortunes, Metem," said Aziel quietly, "and in them is no true disgrace. Even if I had the means to kill myself, it would be a sin; moreover, it might bring another to her death. Therefore, I await my doom, whatever it may be, with such patience as I can, trusting that my sufferings and ignominy may expiate my crimes in the sight of Him whom I renounced. But how come you here, Metem?"

"I came under the safe-conduct of Ithobal who gave me leave to visit you, doubtless for some ends of his own. Have you heard, Prince, that he holds the gates of the city, though as yet no harm has been done to it, and that its inhabitants are crowded within the temple, and upon the heights above; also that in his despair Sakon has fallen on his sword and slain himself?"

"Is it so?" answered Aziel. "Well, Issachar foretold as much. On their own heads be the doom of these devil-worshippers and cowards. Have you any tidings of the lady Elissa?"

"Yes, Prince. She still sits yonder in the tomb, resolute in her purpose, and giving no answer to those who come to reason with her."

As he spoke the guard let fall the front of the tent so that the sunlight flowed into it, revealing Aziel and his twelve companions, each fast in his narrow and shameful prison. "See," said Metem, "do you know the place?"

The prince struggled to his knees, and saw that they were set upon the top of a hill, built up of granite boulders, which rose eighty feet or more from the surface of the plain. Opposite to them at a distance of under a hundred paces was a precipice in the face of which could be seen a cave closed with barred gates of bronze, while between the rocky hill and the precipice ran a road.

"I know it, Metem; there runs the path by which we travelled from the coast, and there is the tomb of Baaltis. Why have we been brought here?"

"The lady Elissa sits behind the bars of yonder tomb whence her view of all that happens upon this mount must be very good indeed," answered Metem with meaning. "Now, can you guess why you were brought here, prince Aziel."

"Is it that she may witness our sufferings under torment?" he asked.

Metem nodded.

"How will they deal with us, Metem?"

"Wait and see," he answered sadly.

As he spoke Ithobal himself appeared followed by certain evil-looking savages. Having greeted Metem courteously he turned to the Hebrew soldiers in the cages and asked them which of their number was most prepared to die.

"I, Ithobal, who am their leader," said Aziel.

"No, Prince," replied Ithobal with a cruel smile, "your time is not yet. Look, there is a man who has been wounded; to put him out of his pain will be a kindness. Slaves, bear that Jew to the edge of the rock, and—as the prince will wish to study a new mode of death—bring his cage also."

The order was obeyed, Aziel being set down upon the very verge of the cliff. Close to him a spur of granite jutted out twenty feet or so from the edge. At the end of the spur a groove was cut and over this groove, suspended by a thin chain from a pole, hung a wedge of pure crystal carefully shaped and polished. While Aziel wondered what evil purpose this stone might serve, the slaves had fastened a fine rope to the cage containing the wounded Hebrew soldier and secured its end. Then they set the rope in the groove of the granite spur, and pushed the cage over the edge of the cliff, so that it dangled in mid-air.

"Now I will explain," said Ithobal. "This is a method of punishment that I have borrowed from those followers of Baal who worship the sun, by means of which Baal claims his own sacrifice, and none are guilty of the victim's blood. You see yonder crystal—well, at any appointed hour, for it can be hung as you will, the rays of the sun shining through it cause the fibres of the grass rope to smoke and smoulder till at length they part and—Baal takes his sacrifice. Should a cloud hide the sun at the appointed hour, then, Baal having spared him, the victim is set free. But, as you will note, at this season of the year there are no clouds.

"What, Prince, have you nothing to say?" he went on, for Aziel had listened in silence to the tale of this devilish device. "Well, learn that it depends upon the lady Elissa yonder whether or not this fate shall be yours. Send now and pray her to save you. Think what it will be to hang as at this moment your servant hangs over that yawning gulf of space, waiting through the long hours till at last you see the little wreaths of smoke begin to curl from the tinder of the cord. Why! before the end found them I have known men go mad, and, like wolves, tear with their teeth at the wooden bars.

"You will not. Then, Metem, do you plead for your friend. Bid the Baaltis look forth at one hour before noon and see the sight of yonder wretch's death, remembering that to-morrow this fate shall be her lover's unless she foregoes her purpose of self-murder and gives herself to me. Nay, no words! an escort shall lead you through the lower city to the gateway of the tomb and there listen to your speech. See that it does not fail you, merchant, unless you also seek to hang in yonder cage. Tell the lady Elissa that to-morrow at sunrise I will come in person for her answer. If she yields, then the prince and his companions shall be set free and with you, Metem, to guide them, be mounted on swift camels to carry them unharmed to their retinue beyond the mountains. But if she will not yield, then—Baal shall take his sacrifice. Begone."

So, having no choice, Metem bowed and went, leaving the caged Aziel upon the edge of the cliff, and the Hebrew soldier hanging from the spur of rock.

Now Aziel roused himself from the horror in which his soul was sunk, and strove to comfort his doomed comrade, praying with him to Heaven.

Slowly as they prayed, the hours drew on till at length, upon the opposite cliff, he saw men whom he knew to be Metem and his escort, approach the mouth of the tomb, and faintly heard him call through the bars of the gateway. Turning himself in his cage, Aziel glanced at the rope, and watched the spot of light born from the burning glass of the crystal creep to its side.

Now the fatal moment was at hand, and Aziel saw a little wreath of smoke rise in the still air and bade his wretched servant close his eyes. Then came the end. Suddenly the taut rope, eaten through by the sun's fire, flew back and the cage with the soldier in it vanished from his sight, while, from far below, rose the sound of a heavy fall, and from the tomb of Baaltis rang the echo of a woman's shriek.

Chapter XVII

"There is Hope"

It was dawn. Ithobal the king stood without the gates of the tomb of Baaltis, the grey light glimmering faintly on his harness, and knocked upon the brazen bars with the handle of his sword.

"Who troubles me now?" said a voice within.

"Lady, it is I, Ithobal, who, as I promised by Metem the Phoenician, am come to learn your will as to the fate of my prisoner, the Prince Aziel. Already he hangs above the gulf, and within one short hour, if you so decree it, he will fall and be dashed to pieces. Or, if you so decree it, he will be set free to return to his own land."

"At what price will he be set free, king Ithobal?"

"Lady, you know the price; it is yourself. Oh! I beseech you, be wise! spare his life and your own. Listen: spare his life, and I will spare this city which lies in the hollow of my hand, and you shall rule it with me."

"You cannot bribe me thus, king Ithobal. My father whom I loved is dead, and shall I give myself to you for the sake of a city and a Faith that would have betrayed me into your hands?"

"Nay, but for the sake of the man to whom you are dear, you shall do even this, Elissa. Think: if you refuse, his blood will be upon your head, and what will you have gained?"

"Death, which I seek, for I weary of the struggle of my days."

"Then end it in my arms, lady. Soon this fancy will escape your mind, and you will remain one of the mightiest queens of men."

Elissa returned no answer, and for a while there was silence.

"Lady," said Ithobal at length, "the sun rises and my servants yonder await a signal."

Then she spoke like one who hesitates.

"Are you not afraid, king Ithobal, to trust your life to a woman won in such a fashion?"

"Nay," answered Ithobal, "for though you say that their fate does not concern you, the lives of all those penned-up thousands are hostages for my own. Should you by chance find a means to stab me unawares, then to-night fire and sword would rage through the city of Zimboe. Nor do I fear the future, since I know well that you who think you hate me now, very soon will learn to love me."

"You promise, king Ithobal, that if I yield myself you will set the prince Aziel free; but how can I believe you who twice have tried to murder him?"

"Doubt me if you will, Elissa, at least, you cannot doubt your own eyes. Look, his road to the sea runs beneath this rock. Come from the tomb and take your stand upon it and you shall see him pass; yes, and should you wish, speak with him in farewell that you may be sure that it is he and alive. Further, I swear to you by my head and honour, that no finger shall be laid upon you till he is gone by, and that no pursuit of him shall be attempted. Now choose."

Again there was silence for a while. Then Elissa spoke in a broken voice.

"King Ithobal, I have chosen. Trusting to your royal word I will stand upon the rock and when I have seen the prince Aziel go by in safety, then, since you desire it, you shall put your arms about me and bear me whither you will. You have conquered me, king Ithobal! Henceforward these lips of mine are yours and no other man's. Give the signal, I pray you, and I will cast aside the dagger and the poison and come out living from this tomb."

Aziel hung in his cage over the abyss of air, awaiting death, and glad to die, because now he was sure that Elissa had refused to purchase his life at the expense of her own surrender. There he hung, dizzy and sick at heart, making his prayer to heaven and waiting the end, while the eagles that would prey upon his shattered flesh swept past him.

Presently, from the opposing cliff, came the sound of a horn blown thrice. Then, while Aziel wondered what this might mean, the cage in which he lay was drawn in gently over the edge of the precipice, and carried down the steeps of the granite hill as it had been carried up them.

At the foot of the hill its covering was torn aside, and he saw before him a caravan of camels, and seated on each camel a comrade of his own. But one camel had no rider, and Metem led it by a rope.

The servants of Ithobal took him from the cage and set him upon this camel, though they did not loosen the bonds about the wrists.

"This is the command of the king," said the captain to Metem "that the arms of the prince Aziel shall remain bound until you have travelled for six hours. Begone in safety, fearing nothing."

"What happens now, Metem," asked Aziel, as the camels strode forward, "and why am I set free who was expecting death? Is this some new artifice of yours, or has the lady Elissa—" and he ceased.

"Upon the word of an honest merchant I cannot tell you, Prince. Yesterday, as I was forced, I gave the message of king Ithobal to the lady Elissa yonder in the tomb. She would answer me only one thing, which she whispered in my ear through the bars of the holy tomb; that if we could escape we should do so, moreover that you must have no fear for her since she also had found a means of escape from Ithobal, and would certainly join us upon the road."

As Metem spoke, the camels passed round the little hill on to the path that ran beneath the tomb of Baaltis. There, standing upon the rock some fifty feet above them, was Elissa, and with her, but at a distance, Ithobal the king.

"Halt, prince Aziel," she called in a clear voice, "and hearken to my farewell. I have bought your life, and the lives of your companions, and you are free, for the road is clear and nothing can overtake the twelve swiftest camels in Zimboe. Go, therefore, and be happy, forgetting no word that has passed my lips. For all my words are true, even to a certain promise which I made you lately by the mouth of Metem, and which I now fulfil—that I would join you on your road lest you should deem me faithless to the troth which I have so often sworn to you.

"King Ithobal, this shape is yours; come now and take your prize. Prince Aziel, my soul is yours, in life it shall companion you, and in death await you. Prince Aziel, I come to you." Then, before he could answer a single word, with one swift and sudden spring she hurled herself from the cliff edge to fall crushed upon the road beneath.

Aziel saw. In his agony he strained so fiercely at the bonds which held him that they burst like rushes. He leapt from the camel and knelt beside Elisa. She was not yet dead, for her eyes were open and her lips stirred.

"I have kept faith, keep it also, Aziel! the story is not yet done," she gasped. Then her life flickered out, and her spirit passed.

Aziel rose from beside the corpse and looked upward. There upon the edge of the rock above him, leaning forward, his eyes blind with horror, stood Ithobal the king. Aziel saw him, and a fury entered into his heart because this man, whose jealous rage and evil doing had bred such woe and caused the death of his beloved still lived upon the earth. By the prince was Metem, who, for once, had no words, and from his hand he snatched a bow, set an arrow on the string and loosed.

The shaft rushed upwards, it smote Ithobal between the joints of his harness so that the point of it sunk through this neck.

"This gift, king Ithobal, from Aziel the Israelite," he cried, as the arrow sped.

For a moment the great man stood still, then he opened his arms wide and of a sudden plunged downward, falling with a crash on the roadway, where he lay dead at the side of dead Elissa.

"The play is played, and the fate fulfilled," cried Metem. "See, the servants of the king speed yonder with their evil tidings; let us away lest we bide here with these two for ever."

"That is my desire," said Aziel.

"A desire which may not be fulfilled," answered Metem. "Come, Prince, since we cannot go without you. Surely you do not wish to sacrifice the lives of all of us as an offering to the great spirit of the lady who is dead. It is one that she would not seek."

Then Aziel knelt down and kissed the brow of the dead Elissa, and went his way, saying no word.

That night, when the darkness fell, the sky behind these travellers grew red with fire.

"Behold the end of the golden city!" said Metem. "Zimboe is food for flames and its children for the sword. Issachar was a prophet indeed, who foretold that it should be so."

Aziel bowed his head, remembering that Issachar had foretold also that for Elissa and for him there was hope beyond the grave. As he thought it, a wind beat upon his brow and through it a soft voice seemed to murmur to his heart:—

"Be of good courage: Beloved, there is hope."

So, turning from the death behind him, this far away forgotten lover set his face to the sea of Life and passed it, and long ago, at his appointed hour, gained its further shore, to be welcomed there by her who watched for him.

And thus, because of the fateful and predestined loves of Aziel the prince, and Elissa the priestess and daughter of Sakon, three thousands years and more ago, the ancient city of Zimboe fell at the hand of king Ithobal and his Tribes, so that to-day there remain of it nothing but a desolate grey tower of stone, and beneath, the crumbling bones of men.

H. Rider Haggard – A Short Biography

Sir Henry Rider Haggard, KBE was born on June 22nd, 1856 at Bradenham in Norfolk, England.

More familiarly known as H. Rider Haggard, he was the eighth of ten children born to Sir William Meybohm Rider Haggard, a barrister (born, incidentally, in St Petersburg, Russia), and Ella Doveton, an author, poet and daughter of a merchant in the East India Trading Company.

Haggard was initially schooled at Garsington Rectory in Oxfordshire where he studied under the tutelage of Reverend H. J. Graham. His elder brothers, who seemed to find more favour with their father, graduated from various private schools whilst Haggard was sent to Ipswich Grammar School, saving his father a considerable sum in fees.

He failed his army entrance exam, and was therefore sent to a private crammer in London in preparation for the entrance exam to the British Foreign Office, which he appears never to have sat. However, it was during his two years in London that Haggard came into contact with a circle of people interested in the study of psychical phenomena and for which he too now developed a life-long interest together with a series of enduring friendships.

In 1875, Haggard's father used his family's connections to send him to Southern Africa to take up an unpaid position as assistant to the secretary to Sir Henry Bulwer, Lieutenant-Governor of the Colony of Natal. In 1876 he was transferred to the staff of Sir Theophilus Shepstone, Special Commissioner for the Transvaal. It was in this role that Haggard was present in Pretoria in April 1877 for the official announcement of the British annexation of the Boer Republic of the Transvaal. The official who had been nominated to read out the Proclamation lost his voice and Haggard was his replacement. It was a moment in history.

Haggard was to remain in the country for six years, during which time he served as Master of the High Court of the Transvaal and an adjutant of the Pretoria Horse.

It was here that he fell in love with Mary Elizabeth "Lilly" Jackson. He hoped to marry her once he obtained more certainty in his career path.

In 1878 he became Registrar of the High Court in the Transvaal and now the time seemed opportune to write to his father to tell him of his hope to marry. The reply from his father was uncompromising. He forbade it until his son had made a proper career for himself.

The following year, 1879, Lily married Frank Archer, a well-to-do banker.

Haggard returned briefly to England to marry a friend of his sister's, Marianna Louisa Margitson, a 21 year old, in 1880, and the couple travelled to Africa together. Haggard's years in Africa had proved, at least on a writing level, rich and inspirational for him, and while still in Natal he wrote two articles for The Gentleman's Magazine describing his experiences.

Moving back to England in (and accounts here differ as to whether it was 1881 or 1882) the couple settled in Ditchingham, Norfolk, Louisa's ancestral home. Later they moved to Kessingland and established connections with the church in Bungay, Suffolk. The marriage produced four children. A son named Jack (who tragically died at age 10 of measles) and three daughters, Angela, Dorothy and Lilias. (Lilias grew to become an author and her father's biographer.)

In England Law was to be the fulcrum of his career. However, although he studied, writing was growing in its appeal to him. His first book, Cetywayo and His White Neighbours, was an account and study of Britain's policies in South Africa.

From this point his career as a writer began to take substantial hold and with it a dramatic shift to fiction. Two years later he published his first fiction, Dawn followed in 1885 by arguably his most popular novel, King Solomon's Mines—detailing the life of the adventurer Allan Quatermain. This was followed the following year, 1886, by She: A History of Adventure, which introduced the female character Ayesha. Both characters, Quatermain and Ayesha, developed a series of books about their adventures.

The study of Law now fell away entirely. He appeared also to have a keen sense of his commercial appreciation. Rather than sell the copyright of his first best-seller, King Solomon's Mines, for a £100 fee he, instead, accepted a 10% royalty. This book is also generally accepted as the first of the Lost World writing genre.

Haggard obviously thought there were many further adventures to tell and it would be hard to find a publisher who would disagree given the start he had made. Sequels soon followed. Allan Quatermain continued his epic and swash-buckling adventures in Africa whilst the sequel to She entitled Ayesha played out her adventures in Tibet. Interestingly Haggard would later extend his characters adventures around the world with Eric Brighteyes, being the basis for an epic Viking romance.

The Haggard family lived at 69 Gunterstone Road in Hammersmith, London, from mid-1885 to mid-1888. It was here that he wrote his most famous works. His time in Africa had given him the experience and atmosphere as well as several observations and friendships of the people who would so influence his fictional characters. Chief among them were the larger-than-life adventurers Frederick Selous and Frederick Russell Burnham. Both were men of Empire and huge ambition as they helped uncover the great mineral wealth of Africa, as well as the ruins of ancient lost civilisations of the continent, such as Great Zimbabwe.

Three of Haggard's books, The Wizard (1896), Black Heart and White Heart; a Zulu Idyll (1896), and Elissa; the Doom of Zimbabwe (1898), are dedicated to Burnham's daughter Nada, the first white child born in Bulawayo; she had been named after Haggard's 1892 book Nada the Lily.

As is typical of the writing of the time his novels contain many of the stereotypes associated with colonialism, yet they also sympathise, to a degree, with the native populations. Africans often play heroic roles in the novels, although the protagonists are more often than not European. The time around the turn of the century was, after all, the great sprint to Empire by many European countries intent on gaining possessions of land, people and resources.

Three of Haggard's novels were written in collaboration with his friend Andrew Lang who shared his interest in the spiritual realm and paranormal phenomena and who was also a greatly admired editor.

Haggard's stories are still widely read today. Ayesha, the female protagonist of She, has been cited as a prototype by psychoanalysts such as Sigmund Freud (in The Interpretation of Dreams) and Carl Jung. Her epithet is, of course, "She Who Must Be Obeyed" and has for decades been used tongue-in-cheek to describe the presumed balance of influence between the sexes.

As a legacy it is easy to establish Haggard, and his pioneering work, as the author of the Lost World branch of writing and its influence of such other writers as Edgar Rice Burroughs, Robert E. Howard and Talbot Mundy. The Allan Quatermain character influenced many 'serials' in Hollywood during the 30s & 40s and can readily be seen as a template for Indiana Jones, the American archaeologist and explorer and huge box office film character.

Years later, when Haggard was a successful novelist, he was contacted by his former love, Lilly Archer, née Jackson. Lily had been deserted by her husband, who had embezzled funds and fled bankrupt to Africa. Haggard installed her and her sons in a house and saw to the children's education. Lilly eventually followed her husband to Africa, where he infected her with syphilis before dying of it himself. Lilly returned to England in late 1907, where Haggard again supported her until her death on April 22nd, 1909.

Haggard also wrote about agricultural and social reform, in part inspired by his experiences in Africa, but also based on what he saw in Europe. By the end of his life, he was adamantly opposed to Bolshevism, a position that he shared with his life-long friend Rudyard Kipling. The two had found friendship upon Kipling's arrival at London in 1889 largely on the strength of their shared opinions.

Haggard was extremely interested in the social affairs of the Country and eager to play a more active part in attempting reform. In 1895 he stood unsuccessfully for Parliament as a Conservative candidate for the Eastern division of Norfolk losing by 198 votes.

Also in 1895 he served on a government commission to examine Salvation Army labour colonies. This, and his heavy involvement in agriculture reform, led to him being a member of several further commissions on land use and related affairs, work that involved several trips to the Colonies and Dominions. This work, in part, helped lead to the passage of the 1909 Development Bill.

In 1911 he served on the Royal Commission examining coastal erosion.

He was an absorbed and dedicated writer of letters to The Times, nearly one hundred were published by them and the bibliography attached below reveals much in the range of subjects he wished to bring attention to.

He was made a Knight Bachelor in 1912 and a Knight Commander of the Order of the British Empire in 1919. Haggard was a member of several clubs including the Athenaeum, Savile, and Authors' clubs.

The district of Rider in British Columbia, Canada, was named in his honour.

Henry Rider Haggard died on May 14th, 1925 at the age of 68. His ashes were buried at Ditchingham Church. His papers are held at the Norfolk Record Office.

The first chapter of his book People of the Mist (1894) is credited with inspiring the 1912 motto of the Royal Air Force (formerly the Royal Flying Corps), Per ardua ad astra. "Through adversity to the stars" (or alternately "Through struggle to the stars") it is also used by other Commonwealth air forces such as the RAAF, RCAF, RNZAF, and the SAAF.

H. Rider Haggard – A Concise Bibliography

Novels
Dawn (1884) Published in three volumes
The Witch's Head (1884) Published in three volumes
King Solomon's Mines (1885) Allan Quatermain series
She: A History of Adventure (1886) Ayesha series
Allan Quatermain (1887) Allan Quatermain series
Jess (1887)
A Tale of Three Lions (1887) Allan Quatermain series
Maiwa's Revenge, or the War of the Little Hand (1888) Allan Quatermain series
Colonel Quaritch, VC (1889) Published in three volumes
Cleopatra (1889)
Beatrice (1890)
The World's Desire (1890) Co-written with Andrew Lang

Eric Brighteyes (1891)
Nada the Lily (1892)
An Heroic Effort (1893)
Montezuma's Daughter (1893)
The People of the Mist (1894)
Heart of the World (1895)
Joan Haste (1895)
The Wizard (1896)
Doctor Therne (1898)
Swallow: A Tale of the Great Trek (1899)
Lysbeth (1901)
Pearl Maiden (1903)
Stella Fregelius: A Tale of Three Destinies (1903)
The Brethren (1904)
Ayesha: The Return of She (1905) Ayesha series
The Way of the Spirit (1906)
Benita (1906)
Fair Margaret (1907)
The Ghost Kings(1908)
The Yellow God (1908)
The Lady of Blossholme (1909)
Morning Star (1910)
Queen Sheba's Ring (1910)
Red Eve (1911)
The Mahatma and the Hare (1911)
Marie (1912) Allan Quatermain series
Child of Storm (1913) Allan Quatermain series
The Wanderer's Necklace (1914)
The Holy Flower (1915) Allan Quatermain series
The Ivory Child (1916) Allan Quatermain series
Finished (1917) Allan Quatermain series]
Love Eternal (1918)
Moon of Israel (1918)
When the World Shook (1919)
The Ancient Allan (1920) Allan Quatermain series
She and Allan (1921) Allan Quatermain series / Ayesha series
The Virgin of the Sun (1922)
Wisdom's Daughter (1923) Ayesha series
Heu-Heu (1924) Allan Quatermain series]
Queen of the Dawn (1925)
The Treasure of the Lake (1926) Allan Quatermain series
Allan and the Ice-Gods (1927) Allan Quatermain series
Mary of Marion Isle (1929)
Belshazzar (1930)

Short Story Collections
Allan's Wife and Other Tales (1889)

Black Heart and White Heart: A Zulu Idyll (1900)
Smith and the Pharaohs (1920)

Publications in Periodicals and Newspapers
A Zulu War-Dance (July 1877) The Gentleman's Magazine
A Visit to the Chief (September 1877) The Gentleman's Magazine
Hydrophobia (letter) (3 November 1885) The Times
The Land Question (letter) (28 April 1886) The Times
About Fiction (February 1887) The Contemporary Review
Mr Rider Haggard and His Critics (letter) (27 April 1887) The Times
Our Position in Cyprus (July 1887) The Contemporary Review
American Copyright (letter) (11 October 1887) The Times
On Going Back (November 1887) Longman's Magazine
Delagoa Bay (letter) (17 December 1887) The Times
South African Policy (letter) (27 December 1887) The Times
Suggested Prologue to a Dramatised Version of She (March 1888) Longman's Magazine
Mr. Meeson's Will (18 June 1888) The Illustrated London News
The Wreck of the Copeland (18 August 1888) The Illustrated London News
Cleopatra (3 December 1888) The Illustrated London News
Hydrophobia and Muzzling (letter) (25 October 1889) The Times
The Annals of Natal (23 November 1889) The Saturday Review
Mummy at St Mary/Woolnoth's (letter) (25 December 1889) The Times
Mummies (letter) (27 December 1889) The Times
The Fate of Swaziland (January 1890) The New Review
In Memoriam (17 May 1890) Thompson's Seasons
American Copyright (letter) (5 June 1890) The Times
Mr Herbert Ward and Mr Stanley (10 November 1890) The Times
Nada the Lily (2 January 1892) The Illustrated London News
A New Argument Against Creation (19 December 1892) The Times
My First Book. Dawn. By H. Rider Haggard (April 1893) The Idler
The Tale of Isandlwana and Rorke's Drift (4 October 1893) The True Story Book
Lobengula (letter) (19 October 1893) The Times
The New Sentiment (letter) (6 November 1893) The Times
Wanted—Imagination   (25 December 1893) The Times
The Fate of Captain Patterson's Party (28 December 1893) The Times
The Three Volume Novel (letter) (27 July 1894) The Times
The Adventures of John Gladwyn Jebb (letter) (30 October 1894) The Times
Agriculture in Norfolk (letter) (30 October 1894) The Times
The Nelson Bazaar (letter) (16 February 1895) The Times
Everything is Peaceful (letter) (20 March 1895) The Times
Lord Kimberley in Norfolk (letter) (17 April 1895) The Times
The East Norfolk Election (letter) (23 July 1895) The Times
The East Norfolk Election (letter) (29 July 1895) The Times
Wilson's Last Fight (7 October 1895) The True Story Book
The Crisis in the Transvaal (letter) (2 January 1896) The Times
The Transvaal Crisis (letter) (13 January 1896) The Times
Jameson's Surrender (letter) (14 March 1896) The Times

The Rinderpest in South Africa (letter) (5 November 1896) The Times
Mr Rider Haggard and Dr Neufeld (letter) (9 January 1899) The Times
Shrinkage of Population in Agricultural Districts (letter) (9 May 1899) The Times
The South African Crisis—An Appeal (letter) (1 July 1899) The Times
Commandant-General Joubert and Mr H Rider Haggard (letter) (8 September 1899) The Times
Anglo-African Writers' Club (17 October 1899) The Times
The War (letter) (25 October 1899) The Times
Farming in 1899 (letter) (22 December 1899) The Times
Farming in 1899 (letter) (1 January 1900) The Times
Settlement of Soldiers in South Africa (letter) (5 May 1900) The Times
1881 and 1900 (letter) (2 October 1900) The Times
Farming in 1900 (letter) (1 January 1901) The Times
Central and Associated Chambers of Agriculture (letter) (6 November 1901) The Times
Small Holdings (letter) (8 November 1901) The Times
Rural England (letter) (4 February 1903) The Times
Mr Rider Haggard on Rural Depopulation (3 May 1903) The Times
Agricultural Distress (letter) (11 June 1903) The Times
The Motor Problem (letter) (24 June 1903) The Times
Fiscal Policy and Agriculture (letter) (16 December 1903) The Times
Telepathy Between a Human Being and a Dog (letter) (21 July 1904) The Times
Telepathy Between a Human Being and a Dog (letter) (9 August 1904) The Times
Mr Rider Haggard on Small Holdings (12 September 1904) The Times
Case L.1139 Dream (October 1904) Journal of the Society for Psychical Research
Mr Rider Haggard on Agriculture (22 October 1904) The Times
Mr Rider Haggard on Rural Housing (27 October 1904) The Times
The Deserted Village (letter) (25 August 1905) The Times
Decrease of Population and the Land (letter) (6 January 1906) The Times
Prevention of Cruelty to Children (3 February 1906) The Times
The New Land and Tenure Bill (letter) (12 March 1906) The Times
Garden City Association (17 March 1906) The Times
Mr H. Rider Haggard on the Zulus (19 May 1906) The Illustrated London News
To Be Proof against British Bullets: A Zulu Incantation (19 May 1906) The Illustrated London News
Housing of the Working Classes (26 June 1906) The Times
Mr Rider Haggard on Small Holdings (4 July 1906) The Times
The Unemployed and Waste City Lands (letter) (19 July 1906) The Times
Mr Rider Haggard on the Transvaal Constitution (7 August 1906) The Times
Vanishing East Anglia (1 September 1906) The Saturday Review
The Land Grabbing at Plaistow (5 September 1906) The Times
The Land Tenure Bill (22 November 1906) The Times
Publishers and the Public (letter) (19 February 1907) The Times
The Careless Children (2 March 1907) The Saturday Review
The Government and the Land (letter) (29 April 1907) The Times
Chambers of Agriculture (2 May 1907) The Times
The Government and the Land (letter) (8 May 1907) The Times
Miss Jebb on Small Holdings (15 June 1907) Country Life
Rural Housing and Sanitation Association (27 June 1907) The Times
St Thomas Hospital Medical School (28 June 1907) The Times
The Land Question (4 July 1907) The Times

Empire Land Settlement by Sir Rider Haggard (December 1916) United Empire
A Journey through Zululand by Sir H Rider Haggard (December 1916) The Windsor Magazine
Mr Wilson's Note. British Publicity (28 December 1916) The Times
Home Produce (letter) (22 February 1917) The Times
The Milk Supply (letter) (11 April 1917) The Times
Corn Production Bill. A National Measure (letter) (13 June 1917) The Times
A Protest and a Plea. Farmers and Meat (letter) (9 October 1917) The Times
Pig-Breeding. A Subject for Municipal Enterprise (letter) (22 February 1918) The Times
The German Colonies. Interests of the Dominions (letter) (5 November 1918) The Times
Light—More Light! (letter) (19 November 1918) The Times
A Great American. Tributes to the Late Mr Roosevelt (letter) (8 January 1919) The Times
Shut the Door (letter) (10 March 1919) The Times
Population and Housing. Emigration v Birth Control (25 March 1919) The Times
The Ex-Kaiser (letter) (11 April 1919) The Times
Empire Birth-Rate. Sir Rider Haggard on Emigration (17 April 1919) The Times
Ex-Service Men Abroad. Warnings from California (letter) (10 May 1919) The Times
Edith Cavell (letter) (16 May 1919) The Times
The Ex-Kaiser. Uncertainties of Trial (letter) (8 July 1919) The Times
Race Suicide Peril. Western Civilization Threatened (11 October 1919) The Times
The British Cinema. Production of Reputable Films (letter) (5 November 1919) The Times
Horrors on the Film. Limits of Publicity (letter) (19 November 1919) The Times
The British Museum (letter) (24 January 1920) The Times
Air Exploration and Empire (letter) (7 February 1920) The Times
The Liberty League. A Campaign Against Bolshevism (letter) (3 March 1920) The Times
Bolshevist Peril. Counter-Propaganda (4 March 1920) The Times
The Empire's Vacant Lands. Settlers and the Food Supply (14 April 1920) The Times
Films and Happy Endings. The Tyranny of a Convention (letter)   (21 April 1921) The Times
Land and its Burdens. Evil of Grinding Taxation (letter) (8 August 1921) The Times
Boy Emigrants (letter) (31 March 1922) The Times
Migration and Morals. Declining Birther Rate (7 April 1922) The Times
Labour Party's Programme. Confiscation and Class Hatred (letter) (28 October 1922) The Times
Efficient Denmark. Keeping the People on the Land (7 December 1922) The Times
The Egyptian Find. Tombs of Eighteenth Dynasty Queens (letter) (19 December 1922) The Times
King Tutankhamen. Reburial in Great Pyramid (letter) (13 February 1923) The Times
The Norfolk Dispute. A Truce while There is Time (letter) (3 April 1923) The Times
Rural Post and Telephone. Minister's Reply to Deputation (19 April 1923) The Times
Liberalism and Land Reform (letter) (1 May 1923) The Times
Small Holdings. Influence of Heredity (letter) (4 July 1923) The Times
Agricultural Parcel Post (26 July 1923) The Times
Country Houses for Sale. Empty East Anglian Mansions (letter) (14 June 1924) The Times
Plight of Agriculture (24 July 1924) The Times
Loans From the British Museum (letter) (30 July 1924) The Times
Zinovieff Letter. Mr MacDonald and a Political Plot (letter) (29 October 1924) The Times
Two Centuries of Publishing. Tributes to Messrs. Longmans (6 November 1924) The Times
Imagination and War (26 November 1924) The Times

Non-Fiction

Cetywayo and His White Neighbours (1882)
A Farmer's Year (1899)
The Last Boer War (1899)
A Winter Pilgrimage (1901)
Rural England (1902)
A Gardener's Year (1905)
The Poor and the Land (1905)
Regeneration (1910)
Rural Denmark (1911)
The Days of My Life (1926)

King Solomon's Mines
This novel has been adapted at least six times. The first version, King Solomon's Mines, directed by Robert Stevenson, premiered in 1937. The best known version premiered in 1950: King Solomon's Mines, directed by Compton Bennett and Andrew Marton, was followed in 1959 by a sequel, Watusi. In 1979 a low-budget version directed by Alvin Rakoff, King Solomon's Treasure, combined both King Solomon's Mines and Allan Quatermain in one story. The 1985 film King Solomon's Mines was a tongue-in-cheek parody of the story, with a 1987 sequel in the same vein, Allan Quatermain and the Lost City of Gold. Around the same time an Australian animated TV film came out, King Solomon's Mines. In 2008 a direct-to-video adaptation, Allan Quatermain and the Temple of Skulls, was released.

She
She has been adapted for the cinema at least ten times, and was one of the earliest films to be made, in 1899 as La Colonne de feu (The Pillar of Fire), by Georges Méliès. A 1911 version starred Marguerite Snow, a British-produced version appeared in 1916, and in 1917 Valeska Suratt appeared in a production for Fox which is lost. In 1925 a silent film of She, starring Betty Blythe, was produced with the active participation of Rider Haggard, who wrote the intertitles. This film combines elements from all the books in the series.

A decade later another cinematic version of the novels was released, featuring Helen Gahagan, Randolph Scott and Nigel Bruce. Unlike the book and the other films, this 1935 version was set in the Arctic, rather than Africa, and depicts the ancient civilisation of the story in an Art Deco style, with music by Max Steiner.

The 1965 film She was produced by Hammer Film Productions; it starred Ursula Andress as Ayesha and John Richardson as her reincarnated love, with Peter Cushing and Bernard Cribbins as other members of the expedition.

In 2001 another adaption was released direct-to-video with Ian Duncan as Leo Vincey, Ophélie Winter as Ayesha and Marie Bäumer as Roxane.

Dawn
The film Dawn was released in 1917, starring Hubert Carter and Annie Esmond.

Jess

This book was filmed in 1912, featuring Marguerite Snow, Florence La Badie and James Cruze, in 1914 with Constance Crawley and Arthur Maude, and in 1917 as Heart and Soul, starring Theda Bara in the title role.

Beatrice
The book was adapted into a 1921 Italian silent drama film called The Stronger Passion, directed by Herbert Brenon and starring Marie Doro and Sandro Salvini.

Swallow
The novel was adapted into a 1922 South African film.

Stella Fregelius
The book was adapted into a 1921 British film, Stella.

Moon of Israel
This novel was the basis of a script by Ladislaus Vajda, for film-director Michael Curtiz in his 1924 Austrian epic known as Die Sklavenkönigin (Queen of the Slaves).